A Tale of
Mallu Love

A Tale of Mallu Love

A Blessed Political Love Story from the Land of India

SUNILLKOLLAM

PARTRIDGE

A Penguin Random House Company

To order additional copies of this book, contact
Partridge India
000 800 10062 62
orders.india@partridgepublishing.com

www.partridgepublishing.com/india

CHAPTER 1

Life is a celebration of relationships. Every relation brings a spring to our life. Like nature, we too patiently wait for the spring to come. In the course between the first and the last feed, we celebrate all kinships. If we rejoice a relation with the pepper of winter, it becomes so memorable.

In my life too, it was a time for celebration when I got an admission into the MA English course of Sree Narayana College, Kollam, since I as well began a new relationship here. The change of seasons is for festivity rather than for consciousness.

It's true, nowadays it is not a much-sought-after course, yet for me it was a moment of cheer. Doing an MA in a regular college is different from doing it in private and parallel institutes. The professional colleges provide us with enough faculty members, a good library with a lot of study materials and Internet browsing facilities, and moreover, a group of brilliant peers.

It was my cherished ambition to get an admission into one of the esteemed colleges under University of Kerala and complete my postgraduate degree. I got that opportunity because of my hard work and profession. I was hard-working in my studies, which were supported by my career of tuition teaching and the genuine interest in both studies and teaching.

While doing my degree, I used to teach in tutorials that helped me very much as a student. I realized that a good teacher should always be a hard-working student. If you want to shine in your studies, do the one thing that your teachers do for you—you prepare yourself to teach you. I did the same practice in my degree course and performed well to secure an open quota seat in PG course in one of the prestigious colleges of my district.

Today was my first day in college. I prayed to my mother, who had always remained my well-wisher even after her demise, before I set out for college. I thought her soul was seeing all this. I simply told her, 'Amma, today my class is going to begin. Bless me, Ma . . .'

It was on 20 July, a sunny day just after the monsoon season, that the classes for the first year of the postgraduate course started in the college. Actually, the course started a month late due to the delayed publication of degree results. The college reopened for the academic year on the first of June itself, so the campus remained active in academic and other activities.

The in and around of the college premises were decorated with flags and banners of different student unions. It reminded me of the entry festival of the government primary schools in Kerala to welcome the newly joined children to the world of letters. The entire entrance bore red festoons and the white flags of SFI, the prominent student union in the college. The entire campus seemed a political battlefield. All these decorations were set up to welcome the newcomers of the different postgraduate courses and make them aware of the presence of these student unions in the campus. The student unions of SFI, AISF, KSU, ABVP, and AIDSO put their huge welcome boards in the main entrance of the college. They looked like the billboards of different liquor brands with the statutory warning: 'Alcohol consumption is injurious to your health.'

The college seemed to me like a historic monument of contemporary value. Before I entered the campus, my memories went back to the great sons of the college who had studied there and proven their lives rewarding, like that of the gifted Malayalam poet Shri O. N. V. Kurup. I never thought a new history of love was going to be written in the four walls of the same college.

As I entered from the main entrance of the college, which is facing the NH 47, the Kollam–Thiruvananthapuram national highway, a group of SFI workers who were distributing pamphlets stopped my bike. I was given a pamphlet. I just ran my eyes over it. It was a request letter to the newcomers to apply for a membership in SFI, the student wing political fraction of the Marxist Communist Party of India. The group identified me as a new kid on the block, and so they approached me.

'I am comrade Anil Prasad, the present college chairman.' The crew leader, wearing a white dhoti and coloured shirt, shook hands with me and introduced himself. 'This is comrade Noushad Parambil, SFI unit president, and next to him is comrade Sandeep Vallikuzhi,' he continued, introducing the entire squad one by one.

I sensed that they could have noticed me at the time of the interview; that was why they gave their introduction before asking anything about me.

After this short introduction, he asked me a series of questions: my name, course, and whereabouts.

I told them, 'I am Nilesh, first-year MA English scholar, and I come from Parippally.'

'You are welcome to the SFI unit of the College. We believe you will be happy to become a member of SFI,' the chairman presumed.

'Sure,' I promised because I was a supporter and believer of left-wing political ideology.

Hence, we parted, agreeing to meet again in class. They moved towards more freshers who were coming towards the campus for canvassing and making them their followers. They knew well that the early birds catch more worms.

I went straight to the college office to collect my ID card. But the office was not yet open. I asked Ramettan, the office peon, who was sitting on the outside bench (with whom I had made an acquaintance at the day of the interview), about the office time to collect the ID. He told me to come in the afternoon.

'Ramettan, where is the first MA English classroom?' I asked him to refresh my acquaintance with him.

'That building, on the third floor,' he answered, pointing to the old academic block.

So I proceeded to the first-year MA classroom.

On my way, I noticed several fragmented groups were roaming around the campus for the purpose of distributing their party membership and some for simply mingling with the newcomers. I took out my cell from my blue jeans' front pocket. Jeans and a half-sleeved shirt were my favourite dress. On that day, I had on faded light-blue jeans and a tucked-in maroon half-sleeved shirt. I looked at the time. I realized I had reached the campus a little earlier on the opening day. I reached the front of a classroom where I read on the board: 'MA English (First Year)'.

I took my maiden look into the classroom. Nobody was in it. I was the first one to enter it. As I put my first step into the classroom, my memory went back to my mother again, who had very much desired to send her sons to college for higher studies but had departed this life before fulfilling all her wish. I closed my eyes for a moment and prayed to her.

It was a neatly furnished and spacious classroom with ten pad chairs for the participants and a table and chair on the dais for the teaching faculty. I felt I was stifling in the stagnant air in the room due to it remaining closed for the last two or three months. All the windows were not yet opened. I went to open all the windows to get more fresh air. One of the western windows brought a lot of fresh air into the room. I stood there for a while to get the breeze. Something was scribbled on the top of the window. I went by it and read the writing. Somebody had named it as the wisdom window; like a wisdom tooth, it remained at the end of the classroom. From the window, one could see the national highway and the adjoining rail track. Both were busy with heavy traffic, a lot of unidentified mob moving up and down the street.

I realized the place was one of the civilized centres on earth as it had experienced and witnessed the interpretation of literary texts of the great language for the last sixty-five years. The four walls of the classroom had heard more than what was written in the textbooks. It was the first college in Kerala where postgraduate courses were started. The same classroom had been provided for first-year MA English batches for all these years, with only certain changes occurring in the infrastructure and facilities inside the classroom.

Memories and olden times had no value in the modern era of business and gain. The management of the college had once decided to shift the college from the campus but later put aside the decision due to public protest. The college was situated on the main highway to the district headquarters and in the centre spot of the township area. The management saw the possibility of better business by putting up a shopping complex or a medical college in the same campus rather than running the age-old courses. The management thought, what were the benefits of providing the land and buildings for such menial courses at a time when Kerala was facing scarcity for land?

I heard on the interview day that someone had observed during a discussion why the class was kept on the third floor, and he gave the reason that it was to avoid the likely disturbances due to students' strikes. The college had a bad name for political strikes since it was the nursery for many big political guns of the state. Yes, the college had churned out a lot of political leaders to the state and is still contributing in this field.

The politics of the state was not based on developing politics but simply management politics—the management of existing systems and resources. The leaders continuously fail to channel the young brilliance of the state. The politics of the state mostly depends on the oratory skill and managing power of the person who is engaged in politics. In India, a politician's essential quality is not his intelligence and ingenious education but his power of oration and divergent energy to combat his opponent and the special skill to gulp public funds. If you are equipped with all these qualities, you are good for the profession. India is the only country in the world where politics is considered a profession and not a service. Even in the secondary school certificates of students, you can see that the column of the father's occupation has the option of 'politics'.

Dynasty is another major factor that determines your political future in the country. I didn't have any of these qualities, yet I decided to join in politics. Sometimes I used to think it myself, why did I want to join in politics? I did not have any creative intelligence to transform the society, so for what?

Anyhow, the college has been serving as the nursery for these promising politicians of the state. So strikes, clashes, agitations, and even political murders were nothing new to the campus.

Nevertheless, the postgraduate classes was never affected by any sort of students' agitation from the beginning history of the college because the PG students did not get involved so much in politics and the college authorities did not send the scholars home after general strikes; their classes would go on as per the schedule.

For me, it was the first regular college. I sat there with a little apprehension because of a new location in my life. After a few minutes' waiting, I came out of the classroom and took an aerial view of the campus.

As I stood there, I prepared a short message in mind to send my mother. 'Ma, I got admission in a college, and my studies will start within a few minutes. Are you happy now?' I sent it to her as I was standing with my elbows resting on the top of the parapet of the third-storey veranda. I was sure she would be happy receiving the message.

Later on, I began to observe the activities in the campus.

While I was enjoying the panoramic view of the campus activities, I noticed a Honda Amaze parking under the banyan tree in the open space between the new and the old buildings. A pretty and charming girl got out from the front seat. A fatherly figure accompanied her to the college office. They were exchanging some talk while walking towards the college office. Till they disappeared into the office, my eyes' 'cameras' captured a live shoot of the scene in a casual manner as I had nothing else to do.

With the spin of time, my classmates began to arrive at around a quarter past nine. The first that came was a group of three girls a few minutes after me into the class. They were in a jolly mood to talk, laugh, and plan something. When they noticed my presence, they came to me.

'Are you in this class?' one among them asked me.

'Yah,' I replied.

'What's your name?' another of them asked.

'Nilesh.'

'Where are you from?' the first one continued her query.

'Parippally.'

'From where did you do your degree?' the third one enquired.

'In distance mode of the University of Kerala.' To avoid further enquiry, I told the details of the course, but it triggered more questions.

'Wow! Then you got admission in merit seat?' the first one wondered.

The cause of her wonder was due to little prospect for getting good marks in correspondence course degree participants of the University of Kerala in any subject.

They shook hands with me and introduced themselves. This trio were alumni of the college—Reshmi, Seemol, and Shilpa—and so familiar with the situation of the college. They did their degree from the same college and got admission for a postgraduate degree also. It seemed there was nothing else to tell about them, so they asked more about me and my studies and family.

A little later, the girl who came with her father also reached the class.

'Are you Professor Sudheesh's daughter?' Reshmi asked her after exchanging introductory smiles. This trio had the details of all the participants in the class.

'Yah! How do you know?'

'We heard that Mr Sudheesh's daughter is also in our batch.'

'Are you not an anchor of *Pranayaragangal* in Asianet Plus?'

'Yes. Have you ever watched it?' the girl asked.

'On Sundays and holidays.'

'How do you find it?'

'A nice programme.'

She was Shalini Sudheesh. Her father was a reader of the Department of Political Science. He had taught our alumni the subsidiary paper of political science in their degree course.

She was a former BSc Polymer Chemistry student of Government Women's College, Trivandrum. Now she abandoned science and joined literature because she thought it would help her in her profession of anchoring. Within a few minutes, the trio extracted this and more information about her.

In the meantime, a total of six beauties occupied their chairs. As time progressed, it was difficult for me to identify who were my classmates and who were there to sell their politics to us because the class was filled with a crowd of student politicians and seniors.

The last that came were Apsy and Robin Varghese, with whom I had made acquaintance during the interview time last week. We refreshed our acquaintance once again. After a few words exchanged with the new arrivals, Reshmi announced that the quorum was full. But one chair was left vacant. Apsy asked about it. Seemol gave the reason for the vacant chair. The seat was vacant due to the absence of an applicant from the reserved category of scheduled caste and scheduled tribe. If there would be no applicant from the category, it would remain vacant for the entire course's period; she gave this as a clarification of her observation.

At nine thirty, an electronic bell rang for the class. Still the seniors were roaming around the classes, introducing themselves to the newcomers, and they were in the hunt for the most attractive figures among the novices. It was the time for the senior gents to hunt for their female partners. It was a period of plenty for them—plenty of 'colours' to choose from. The girls bring a spring to the college.

The first one hour was lectured by leaders of different student union groups who introduced themselves and, in a very friendly manner, interacted with all of us.

Naveen was one among the seniors that, along with Chippy, was roaming around the classes and spreading some news to their juniors. They were known in the campus as the antilove duo. They had got the name time back when they joined in this college for their degree course. They were the representatives of the new-generation friendship. They used to eat together, sit together, sing together, share the same e-mail ID, and they knew the passwords of each other's social sites and Internet banking accounts; they also travel together, watch films together, and read the same books together, yet they are not lovers. Sometimes they walk around the campus with their arms around each other's shoulders like Romeo and Juliet, yet they were not Romeo or Juliet.

Naveen was the class representative of last year's first-year MA English batch. They were dynamic activists of SFI. They came to our class to ask me about the college chairman's enquiry on my entry into SFI.

'Are you going to be loyal to SFI?' He asked about my interest in campus politics.

I gave him a positive reply not because of interest in students' politics but because of my interest in the ideology of communist socialism even though it requires some updating in the present situation of the society. Kerala had the first elected communist government in the world, but the communism in Kerala is a form of democratic socialism and not the Marxist-Leninist one. In the beginning, working-class socialism worked out in the state and the communist party reigned. In the present scenario, the working class has disappeared from the society; they have formed trade unions to do organized work. As a consequence, physical labour was diminished, and skilled labour was generated. The scarcity of unskilled labourers increased in the state, and that promoted immigration of labourers from other states. The reverse exploitation of work donor by the working class decreased the industries in the state; the worst affected category of the trend remained the educated youths, and there are no more landlords existing in the state to revolt against them for a revolution. Yet my hope in communism rested in a classless and godless society, so I supported the party's ideology.

'We need a representative from your class. Are you willing to contest in the upcoming college elections?' Naveen further enquired.

'I will give my consent tomorrow,' I replied.

They were hunting for class reps from the various first-year MA batches on the upcoming college elections in the month of August. As our talk progressed, some more chairs brought to the class followed by a group of faculty members came to our classroom. When they came in, the political activists left the classroom. The coordinator of the programme, Professor Meera, introduced a guest to us.

For the opening ceremony of our class, the college authorities had welcomed the former principal of the college, who was known as Prof. Shakespeare Ravindran, to handle the opening slot. The faculty members sat in the last row of the class as an honour to the distinguished guest. He was an expert of Shakespearean literature. He told us that for him Shakespeare's dramas were like *Ramayana*. He asserted that not even a single day in his whole life had gone without reading at least a page of Shakespeare. He did not feel repetition a bore in the case of the master of all literatures.

First we felt that somebody had given him 'hand poison' in Shakespearean literature. When he entered into the serious part of the discussion, I switched on the recording key of my mobile. I thought it would be useful for me in my tuition classes. From eleven to one thirty, he interacted with us on the rereading of Shakespearean literature. All Shakespearean characters—from Falstaff to the historical figure, King Henry, and the most tragic hero, Hamlet, and the despairing Desdemona—got new attire in his elucidation.

The slot would really remain as an energy booster for the entire lot till the end of the course. He really made a lasting impression on us. He made all of us his fans within the one slot. Each and every one, including all the faculty members, gave him honour by attending the entire session in a very interactive way. The two-and-a-half-hour class flew by with the easiness of drinking a cup of hot cardamom tea.

The afternoon slot started a little late due to the overlapping of the previous session.

In the afternoon, Madam Meera came with three members of her teaching team. The session was an eye-opening ceremony for the participants. She introduced us to the available teaching faculties and their concerned papers to deal with us. Later she demanded a self-introductory speech from every participant.

Before our introductory function started, she demanded, 'I need an anchor for this function. One can come over here and anchor this function because we need a detailed personal description of our participants.'

Everyone hesitated to go on the dais. Then she herself called the name of Shalini Sudheesh to take the charge of an anchor. The professor welcomed her to the dais, and all of us gave her a big round of applause.

Shalini began by thanking the madam for the honour of calling her for self-introduction and providing the anchoring role for the introductory function. She was already a celebrity among us. She introduced herself and gave a brief summary of her family. She preferred to say why she had chosen literature as her main subject as being mainly due to her present profession. She finished her explanation by citing personal choice as the reason behind choosing the college for her studies.

Being the anchor of the eye-opening ceremony, she requested each and every participant to give a detailed introduction of themselves. She began to welcome us on the dais in the order of our sitting positions.

One by one, we went to introduce ourselves—all the details about personal interests, degree course, future plans, family background, etc. Those who did not give their family background and future prospects were cross-questioned by the anchor. She was really performing her role as an expert anchor.

My turn came. I went up to the dais and introduced myself in my mother tongue. I thought an introduction in mother tongue would be safe for me. I didn't have any stage fright as I had the experience of teaching in tutorial colleges. Shalini took the role of an interviewer and asked me several questions on my personal and professional choice in life.

'Tell us, Mr Nilesh, why didn't you join in a college for your graduation? Is there any particular reason behind it?' she asked me after listening to my brief introduction.

After a short pause, I replied, 'First reason, I didn't get direct admission in the allotment for English literature anywhere. And the second reason was I myself had to work to support my studies.'

'What about your family?'

'Parents are no more, and I have only a brother.'

'What do you do in your free time?'

'I am a parallel college teacher, so teaching and preparations for teaching are the things that I do in my free time.'

'Which classes do you teach?'

'From Plus Two to undergraduate tuition students.'

'Do you have any aversion to English?' she asked the question because my speech was entirely in my mother tongue.

But to this question, I replied in English, 'Nothing like that, but I feel more comfortable with my mother tongue, that's all.'

She showed her superiority in handling situations like these and thanked me for the frank answer.

I was relieved after my turn on the dais. I got back into my seat.

Next was Apsy's turn. He made us all laugh with his high-pitched voice and the pinch of comedy with Shalini.

Then next came an arresting beauty from the entire pack, and she introduced herself as Nimmy Nandan. I took a comprehensive look at her only then. She was a breathtaking beauty with a gentle smile on her face. She looked like a sculpture chiselled out of sandalwood by the great sculptor Brahma. She was a perfect and amazing girl with a mesmerizing dazzle on her eyes, which could make any male heart astounded.

I was captivated by her beauty and mildness. Before she came on the dais, I had never noticed her. Where had she been? Why didn't I take her in earlier? I did not know.

She introduced herself so charmingly, and her gestures had a magnetizing power on me. She stole our hearts with her gentleness and modesty. I was dazzled by her beauty and warm smile. After the wonderful girl's appearance, what was going on there was only a namesake ceremony for me.

There were two more left to deliver their introduction. They too were welcomed. After that, the faculty members wished all of us good and interactive classes that we would get for the entire session.

The last address was from the co-coordinator of the course, who commented on our introductory function as an interesting one and observed that it helped them to know the participants intimately; after her address, she called it a day.

Before leaving the classroom, I asked Robin, 'Are you coming to Kottiyam?'

'No, thanks. I am moving to Chinnakada.' He excused himself.

The entire batch dispatched for the first day at around three thirty in the afternoon. Each one left on their own way, promising to meet tomorrow for the class.

I felt I was going to celebrate my life here with friends, teachers, studies, and a little bit of politics.

CHAPTER 2

From the college, I instantly went to Pournami Tutorial at Kottiyam. I had an evening class there. On my way back home, I had a one-hour class for the Plus Two students. Today I reached there a little bit earlier than usual.

'How was the opening day in the college?' Dileep Kumar, the director of the institute, asked me while we waited for the tea from the tea stall in front of the tutorial.

'A memorable one.' I gave him a short description of the class of Professor Shakespeare Ravindran while taking tea.

After this casual talk with him, I indulged in my preparation for teaching.

Today I had to teach 'A thing of beauty', a poetic excerpt from 'Endymion' written by John Keats. I took my reference text from my bag and revised the references in the poem quickly. I revisualized the previous class and prepared thoroughly for the presentation because most of these students had a background of English as a medium, so I thought I need a foolproof preparation. At four thirty, I went to the class. Even though there was a little lack of interaction, I took the class very interestingly for one hour. The English batch contained around eighty students in a class, so a highly interactive class was not possible here. Yet I felt I was so confident to handle the class in an interesting way that's possible. The motivational part of the poem itself was a great success, and I felt like celebrating the poem along with my students.

After the class, Dileep Sir (we, the tutorial staff, called one another by adding the word 'sir' to with our names to get self-respect among us because the general public never consider this category of teachers as real teachers) paid me for the day and told me the next schedule of class. I took it and proceeded straight to my home.

On my way home, I took a parcel of chapatti and chicken fry for supper from the Moon City Hotel at the Parippally Junction. Today I did not have the mood for preparing dinner. At home, I took a bath and later listened concurrently to the news stories of Arnab Goswami of Times Now and Nikesh of the Reporter channel for some time while having my night meal. Afterwards, I started preparation for the next day's class for the fifth-semester BA English students. I spent more time on preparations for teaching than self-study.

Along with studying, I taught in four parallel institutions at different places; that was the only source of income for me.

Teaching needed more preparation and thorough knowledge because a teacher should show mastery in his topic in tutorial classes to survive there. Student demand for a teacher increases his value in the tutorial field and will reflect in his remuneration. Another reason is that a teacher can make all his students his fans. So I had to work hard to get the meanings in between the lines and the different possible interpretations of characters and situations.

It was at this stage that I accepted the immediate need of a laptop and broadband Internet connection for easy access of study materials at home. For the same purpose, I had joined a monthly instalment chitty scheme in KSFE, a Kerala government financial institute, for the sum of one lakh rupees. If the lot was drawn in my favour, I would get 70,000 rupees in advance; with that, I could manage my present needs. I had to pay back the amount in 100 monthly instalments. But even after eight months of waiting, the lot was not drawn in my favour. Yet I hoped that one day my turn would come. Now I put my dream aside and went on to my preparation fast.

At ten thirty, my bed welcomed me in sharing with her.

On the bed, I recalled the day. The girl's picture came up in my mind's window like a pop-up screen. The day was so special for me. I thought I too began to celebrate my life. Politics and a little bit of love accompanied my feelings as the college course began.

A few days later in college, I met Naveen in the morning and informed him of my consent for the contest in the college elections. He welcomed it and assured me that they would consider my candidature.

Politics and love are two different things. A politician can't be a good lover. Or a good lover can't be a politician. Love goes to one, and politics goes to the other. How could I manage these two opposite poles?

Days passed as usual with the routine works except for one thing—my attraction towards Nimmy that increased a lot. But I hid my feelings from her. There were megabytes of differences between us, yet hope was not ready to depart from my mind. I did not know anything about her family. Knowing about her family is important because marriage in India is a family issue; it is not a matter between the man and the woman who get married.

One day after noon, she went to the wisdom window. A little breeze lifted up her hair that had fallen over her eyes. Her eyes were like a deep sea in which I could perceive my own realm. I beheld them like a suicide looks into the depth of his own grave eyes just before he commits suicide. I witnessed a whirlpool in them. I would like to glide into the swirl of her eyes. They seemed like a bowl full of peace and love for me.

I saw in her eyes a soft typhoon. It damaged a larger part of my heart that I could not repair myself anymore in the coming days of my college life. I realized later that the typhoon was really a typhoon of love. During the following days, the tropical cyclone of love brought strong winds, rain, and thunder in my little heart. I could no more stand aright.

During one of such observations, I noticed her eyelids shut down upon her pearly eyes, like the waves of the sea on its oceanfront. Her flowery, weighty locks created a fence to her eyes, which keep the invaders out of reach of the vicinity of her eyes. Those eyes, I thought, could alter a humble man into a poet, a devotee, or a lunatic. If the eyes are perfect, then each speck of the human can only be perfect as well. Actually, Nimmy was such an attractive beauty, and her dealings with us were much more perfect than her beauty that any man would gravely like to possess her.

A man's life and thoughts always revolve around a woman, like the moon to the earth. Her body and soul are ever present in a man's mind. Her beauty, grace, and femininity transport him into another world. Masculinity is only to surrender before a woman's body and soul. The woman is the most gorgeous and magnificent creation in the universe to a man, and she always would be. Such a creation was this girl to me. She had a pair of angelic eyes. Her eyes and smile transformed me into the state of a lunatic lover.

A man comes from a woman and will go back to her, and until that takes place, he lives in orbit around the feminine body and soul. I too began to feel like that. I remembered the first day in college and Nimmy's introductory speech. Really, I had heard nothing of her introduction. I was really lost in her eyes. I couldn't remember how the day's proceedings came to an end so quickly. When I left on that very first day of college, romance had its clutches on me as cruelly as it made blood spill from my heart.

CHAPTER 3

Going to the college was something of a thrill for me. My studies, the girl I met, my teaching, and my loneliness made my life a full circle. Every day my life began with teaching, sustained with studying and making friendship with the girl, and ended in loneliness. I left my home at six thirty in the morning and came back at six thirty in the evening. In between the time phase, I had to turn in many roles in the same attire. I would be a tuition teacher from seven to nine in the morning; from nine thirty to four, a scholar and an aspirant lover of the girl; and again in the evening, a tuition teacher. Outside home, life was so busy for me, and at the end of the day, I had utter loneliness at home.

At home I shared my evenings with my virtual friends—TV anchors and the photos of my parents which hung on the walls of my bedroom. Another source of interaction at home was with the characters of the texts that I read.

Yet another source of interaction was my cell phone, Sony Experia, which was a gift from my brother who was working in a Gulf country. Six months ago, he sent it for me through one of his friends. I usually received on my cell phone the calls for tutorials to fix the date and time of classes, calls from some local friends to enquire about something, calls from my Chettayi who used to call on alternate Friday evenings to keep in touch with his younger one, Facebook postings of my friends, etc. These activities filled up my interactive life at home.

Teaching was necessary for me to make both ends meet together. In the beginning, time management was a problem for me because one of the tuition centres where I used to go was situated along a road with a private-bus route. Travelling in a private bus took more time than travelling in highway routes. That was why I bought a new bike, the 125cc Hero's Glamour, last year. All the earnings from the last two years had not been enough to buy it, so I had to pledge its RC book to a private financer. Last year, as its cash credit was completed, the private financer then released the RC book. When it was completed, I had joined the KSFE chitty for one lakh rupees with the purpose of buying a laptop and broadband connection. The bike became an indivisible part of my life. Wherever I had to go, if it's within a limit of a fifty-kilometre radius, I rode on it. Even in college, I went on my bike. It was a distance of forty minutes' casual ride from my home. The bike was my medium of travel now. The main advantage was that a lot of time was saved, and it made me punctual at tutorials and now in college too.

The time for the college elections was fast approaching. I did not get a word about my candidature from the SFI unit of the college. A few days before the declaration of elections, I went to meet Naveen and asked him about it.

He told me, 'You already gave us your consent. If there is any opposition from your class, it will go for election. Otherwise, you will be unanimously elected as class rep for SFI.'

In the history of the college, the majority of the winners had been from the SFI, so it gave me confidence to contest. A class rep generally needn't get involved in all political strikes and activities of the student unions. So I thought it would not turn out to be difficult for me. In advance, I told the SFI unit secretary, Kavuvila Anil, about my likely less initiative in political issues of the student union as I had to manage my own affairs. He agreed to it and provided me the two-rupee membership slip, which was valid only for a period of two years in the student union. I was also made a subscriber of *Student Struggle*, the official publication of SFI, after paying 150 rupees for the yearly subscription.

In the class, all of us had become friends so quickly. Within one month, everyone got the freedom to talk freely with one another. Even the faculty members commented on our socializing skill. Robin Varghees, Apsy, and I made a good trio in the class. As we had enough to share and choose from in the matter of girls, the ego clash was less than one would have expected. We discussed and shared everything among us. So we became solid friends quickly.

In advance, I gave the intimation to them on my passion for Nimmy. They gave their word to me in this regard.

Days passed merrily. I celebrated every day like a festive day. Every day I got something memorable from my class to cherish in my mind. A movement or dialogue from Nimmy was enough for me to make the day memorable. If she laughed with me over my jokes, it gave me a lot of pleasure.

Whenever I got an opportunity to help Nimmy, I did it with a lot of pleasure. She also began to observe my concern over her matters.

Lunch break was the time of our chat. We discussed on all matters, including literature, films, politics, and science, during the break. One day we discussed the discovery of the world's smallest FM radio by the Columbia University professors. The invention of graphene, a single-atom layer of carbon, is the world's strongest material and also has electrical properties superior to silicon. But our discussion was its possibilities of being used in human bodies as a human index card to record all the particulars of a person, including date of birth, blood group, nationality, voting rights, etc. His movements and whereabouts would be recorded in the satellite device if it has data-sharing connection. If so, the crimes can be kept in check. Beyond literature, we used to discuss matters like this in the recess period.

Another talk was usually on the newly released films and our constructive criticism of them.

During these discussion times, we sat in a circle like a group activity period in a high school classroom. In the beginning, Nimmy used to sit at the end of the circle. Later on, she came to sit on the adjacent side of my seat. A lady's trust in a man is the foundation stone of love. I had to win her trust if I want to win her over. If I could establish this trust, she would take me as her trustee. I was aware of the fact that I could not be childish in any circumstance to her or to anybody in the class. Being childlike is a good trend, but childishness may abridge the intimacy between us, my common sense told me.

One Friday afternoon when the class was vacant, every one engaged in their own business. Reshmi and Seemol were dozing off over the writing pads on their chairs. Apsy and Robin were engaged in preparing their paper for presentation work. Shilpa and Shalini were in the library. Fatima was busy with her Facebook updates. It was the first time my eyes tangled with Nimmy's when she looked up from her perusal of a material on the critical study of love in John Donne's poetry. I found a coral reef in the shallow area of her eyes, where colourful fishes rode among the coral heights. Her eyes really mesmerized me like the mother's nipples to a newborn child.

It was something more than the mere meeting of our eyes. Sometimes the sense sees more than what we see. She kept her eyes for a minute on mine. I winked both my eyes to realize the situation. With a curious smile, she said 'Hello, what happened' with a full stop and not with a question mark. I just smiled and gestured it away. That was the first sign of love I tried to transmit from my eyes to hers.

A man chases a woman until she catches him. Could I put this into practice?

Love starts not in ordinary but something unusual and out of the way. Our love was still in the air. We could not open our minds to each other. Our eyes knew. Our hearts knew. Our lips knew. We were in love, but we didn't know about it. We never spoke about it. We kept on silent about our love. At least she kept on silent. No, we kept on silent. Love is a thing that needs exposure; only then does it get its fragrance and sweetness.

Sometimes the heart sees what is invisible to the eye, my heart told me.

I began to ride my daily life on the healthy fuel that is love. Love has the competence to give more mileage and smile in life. Every minute of my life was filled with her thoughts.

She remained as a high-megapixel camera for me that captured all the frozen moments I spent in the campus with her.

When she smiled, a hundred roses blossomed in the garden of her eyes, which spread sweet aroma in the air to entice the bees in my heart.

I couldn't simply open my will to her because of the sincerity and charm in her.

Robin one day told me to speak frankly with her about my attraction to her. But I thought that once rejected, I could not approach her again. Love is chemistry. Before the mix is made, the ingredients should be put in accurate and essential quantities. I was trying to put all the components together in a harmonious way to create the desired result of love in her than a hasty mess.

She was a perfect girl. She was a glory of god, a gift to earth from the abode of him. Sometimes veracity is more arresting than fiction. I saw in her an unpretentious and modest nature of a country girl. On the first day itself at the college, I had noticed her. Why did I notice her? I didn't know. Perhaps it was simply because of the infatuation towards girls. No, not at all. It was something more than a mere obsession, but I could not put it into words.

The modest beauty that had faded in the new-generation girls might have been seen in her, and that might be cause of her charm. I wanted to make enough splendid situations to talk and mingle with her. Display of excellence in my studies was one of them. I began to do hard work in my studies to triumph over her. The attraction I had towards her began to benefit me in this way. Anyhow, I was resolute to carry it on to further heights.

I wished for having a superhuman power of a Bollywood hero in me to make her love me. In films, love happens within seconds. Why didn't it happen in real life? I wondered.

CHAPTER 4

August was the month of the college union elections, and I was busy with student union works. I stood as the class representative of our class on behalf of SFI. Usually, I had to work with other members of the college unit of SFI for meeting students and pleading for their votes for the party. I asked Nimmy for lecture notes for my missed classes. She gave me notes without any reluctance. She later began to prepare a copy for me too. I thanked her and my friends for the help they extended to me.

I posted photos and videos in my Facebook to all my colleagues, pleading for their votes. Social media can play a good role in the minds of youngsters. Shares and likes, as well as positive and negative comments, began to appear from party workers and well-wishers and some unknown people. Every day I made a new post in my account, pleading for the victory of my party.

Till the last day of submission of nominations for the class representative for the first-year MA English batch, no nomination reached other than mine.

My first contest in life was successful. I was unopposed in the class and elected unanimously before the actual election process. The student unions of KSU and ABVP had tried their best to make it a contest, but they did not get any supportive candidate. The ABVP union had approached Robin and Shalini Sudheesh and even Nimmy to make them its candidate. But they refused to do so, saying they had no interest in politics.

As we were celebrating my election victory in our classroom after the lunch break, my cell rang. I went to the wisdom widow to attend it.

'Is this Nilesh?'

'Yes, who is speaking?'

'It's from KSFE Parippally. Your chitty on 03-87/26 was drawn in favour of you. You can collect the money on the same date next month.'

'Okay. Okay. Okay.'

I came back to the celebration group and announced my second win on the same day. Life is sometimes like that. If it starts giving you something, it comes in a row; if there is nothing, there will be nothing at all.

They demanded a treat. I assured them the treat would be at Jerome Nagar on the evening of the same day next month.

'Why next month? We want the party today itself,' Apsy remarked.

I told them I would only get the money next month, and with the money, I had to purchase a laptop from Jerome Centre. So we, the entire class, would go there and buy the laptop, and after that would be the treat. Everyone agreed to it.

Meanwhile, I thought of applying for the BSNL Broadband Internet connection. Now one more entertainment was going to reach my home in the form of the World Wide Web. I thought it would be so helpful to me in preparing my notes and PowerPoint presentations for my tuition students. It would be a great booster to my professional as well as learning life.

Now I realized one more new responsibility came over to me as the class rep. If life is busy, loneliness has no role to play in it. I decided to do something for the class. Before the new student council meeting was held by the college management committee, I discussed the matter with my classmates, and we collectively decided to demand for a supplementary interactive whiteboard with an overhead projector and browsing facility (other than the traditional blackboard for our class) and a language lab with Internet connection for the improvement of spoken skill of the junior classes. When the principal and management called the sitting, I put forward our demands, and they agreed to take it positively.

As class rep, I got more chance to mingle with my mates and the teaching faculty.

The race for her continued.

The time of college elections had provided the opportunity to share study materials with Nimmy.

I was determined to find an eternal place in her heart by being the best guy that she had ever seen. The way to a girl's heart is through her ears. If I could attract her through my words, I would win her. Naturally being a decent, candid, and polite lad, I was her choice for study discussions. Whenever I got free time, I had the habit of using the university's information centre library for reference textbooks. It provided me a really good collection of rare references and critical study materials. The university's centre library usually functioned from two thirty in the afternoon to seven thirty in the evening. Whenever I had no other engagements, I spent two hours there. Whatever study material I got from there or from the search engines of the Internet, I would share them with her.

Sometimes I would prepare notes and send them to her through e-mails or WhatsApp via the CamScanner application in my cell. If I missed any class, she would prepare the lecture notes and share it with me. Thus, little by little our camaraderie progressed.

After a few months, she became an active follower of my Twitter account since I would tweet on our syllabus' topics. Her follow-up encouraged me to tweet more and more.

Even though Nimmy and I were good friends, our love was still in the corner. I knew nothing of her internal psyche. Either I did not have the guts to frankly speak to her about my desire or I kept it as a secret in my mind because of the fear of rejection. I was in the throes of pain similar to that of a seven-month-pregnant woman waiting to deliver her first twin babies. Such a pregnant mother sometimes feels labour pains at the seventh month. My pain was similar to it—a sweet pain, but an unbearable one. My mind did not have the health to deliver the love infant, I realized. A major surgical treatment was necessary to pull the love out.

It could be unbearable for me if I did not get her love.

To add oil to the burning fire, she often reminded me of her liking for an arranged marriage. She once observed that she would never accept a proposal of love from her friends. It was a heart-rending remark that I heard from her. Yet I never lost hope. Hope is the only thing that pulls our life forwards.

For me, being loved by a girl was not at all a Herculean task. I could focus on other girls in the college; most of them were waiting for a male friend. Some tuition students had interest in me, and one or two had expressed it to me on quite a few occasions because most of these girls considered me as their friend or a senior mate. In tutorials, a love affair between a teacher and a student took place sometimes. But I didn't want to support it. I respected teaching like a noble profession even though it was tuition teaching. For me love was winning the girl whom I loved.

A man's best behaviour comes out in front of his awaiting sweetheart. But I had to be good at all situations in my life. My teaching profession gave me ample self-respect from my teenage onwards.

I became more conscious of my dress and hairstyle. My total appearance began to change. The situations in our life would define our fashion. I realized that the trail steps to a splendid girl's passion were not built with bricks but with thorns. So one can call love a rose; it resides in thorns.

She seemed to me a medicine for any kind of pain. But there would be no medicine available in the whole world if she would reject me! I constantly kept the fear of rejection from her for many reasons.

I thought about different ways by which I could make her love me. Yet some sound out in my mind, whether I was worthy of such a girl. Her external gaze told me that she was brought up in an aristocratic family of high profile.

Mine was a poor background at home. I didn't even have a decent bed in my house to share in with her. My only wealth was the good memories of my mother aside from the material wealth of the home where I was staying, which was only a structure of a house. My mother was everything to me. At the time when I had been doing my second year of BA, she had died of a cardiac arrest.

My mother was Savithri. I used to call her Savithri Amma at moments of affection and when she was in a balanced state of mind. She was a little eccentric, no doubt, but she always recognized my needs and necessities. She used to cook something for me every day, like a cup of porridge, a curry of jackfruit seeds with spinach and coconut, etc. Whatever it would be, I used to have it as a tasty feast; I did not have any complaint ever.

If I would say more about my mother, it would be that she was a science graduate. Yet she used to wear her sari in a careless manner that gave her a shaggy look of an illiterate woman. Still I recognized her as a widower mother. I kept in mind one such incident in her life. One day she went to the bank to encash her property by pledging it to the cooperative society bank. The bank manager was really taken aback by the style in which she put her signature on the bank documents. Yes, she became crazy after my father's death. It was a real blow to her, and after that, she would never come back to normalcy. He died ten years ago at her age of 42, a good age for a woman to need her life partner mentally and biologically. At that time, I was only a fifth-class student. My elder brother, who was at eighth standard, and I could not recognize the depth of her loss.

My brother was the only blood relation I had now. He went to the Gulf country of Qatar as a sales executive in a paint company. He was older than me by four years. I used to call him Chettayi. He was a self-indulged young man who completed his schooling from the village high school and left studying forever. He was a silent observer of life and had developed the aspiration of going to a Gulf country during his high school days. The large number of Gulf-goers from our area captivated him to the desert countries of UAE. Most of them migrated to these oil-exporting countries as labourers, a few for official works, and some to start business centres.

Currently, engineers, IT professionals, skilled labourers, and medical staff would also go to these Gulf regions because of the expectation of a tall pay from these countries.

Once you went to a Gulf country, you would get the name of a Gulf man, a credit and honour among village folk as well as in the marriage market. The life experiences from these oil-rich countries turned the lives and fortune of most of these jobseekers to a better posture. It usually attracted the coming generations also to go and work there and come back with enough money in hand. They usually think it is better to go abroad and lead a decent life than consider the silly sentiments of family, jibing the ruling governments for not providing a better living in their own birth lands.

Nowadays, the so-called Arabian companies pay salaries that, according to the exchange rate, is of competitive value to the Indian money and Indian salary. So the benefit of working in the desert lands has diminished to certain ill health at the time of retirement. Yet people used to go because there is no opportunity to work in their homeland. We are the victims of foreign exploitation of our workforce. We could not start a trade union in foreign soil, so we work hard and get whatever they give us. The migrating youth wanted only one thing— that their family would live in decent comfort back at home.

Recently, things were changed a lot. The villagers started to earn more money than the Gulf-goers. The real estate business in the area made the youths into money-makers. The setting up of national ESIC's medical college in the area boosted the land price ten to fifty times higher than the previous year's price. Those who had land or those who had recently bought land in these areas became millionaires. So the Gulf influence got a little diminished in the last few years.

A truck full of middlemen used to camp in the area to traffic the properties of the area. They were seen like a band of flies drifting around a well-ripened jackfruit. From morning till night, they would roam around the area. Two of them, Avlad and Sajeev, approached me and offered a dream price of four lakhs rupees per cent for my property. We had a twelve-cent land in the area. It was situated half a kilometre away from the ESIC Junction, the proposed medical college centre. I told them that if I had a wish to sell, I would inform them. They knew well that it was impossible for me and my brother to leave the land. Our father and mother were cremated in the same soil. Our attachment with the soil and the flora was beyond words. Yet they wanted to know our decision on our property. They never left a stone unturned in this area.

Yesterday, I got the money from KSFE and put it into my account. I had already given the security documents to the finance company for the money. I had promised my class a treat on the day of payment.

The next day at the college, I invited all of them to Jerome Nagar at Chinnakada. We requested Madam Meera to let us out one hour before for the get-together, and she granted our request. The entire batch went to Quilon Laps to choose a laptop for me. They chose an HP Elitebook 8440p i5 for me. It was Nimmy's selection, so I liked it very much.

After the purchase, we went to the Ice World Cookies to celebrate the day.

Back at home, I realized that life is a progressive stepladder—step-by-step improvement in everything. The steps in my life also were witnessing advancement in the matter of material wealth as well as my love for the girl—even though her love was delayed somewhere.

The next day itself, I applied for a BSNL landline with 3G broadband Internet connection. I deposited an amount of 2,500 rupees for the Internet accessories with a Wi-Fi booster. On the next day, they provided the connection in my house.

The Internet opened a new world in my home even though it cost 500 rupees per month, which was an extra burden for me. I decided to maintain it because it could provide me more benefits than the money.

CHAPTER 5

The money I got from tutorials as my wage were used to spend for three things—dress, books, and food—other than the monthly instalment fees to KSFE and the telephone charges. In most of the occasions, I had to eat out as I was hectic with study matters. After my admission in college, cooking by myself was a rare thing for me. Truly, I did not have the time. Yet often I tried to cook my dinner myself.

One of my distant relatives was a resident in my neighbourhood. Our houses were only a cakewalk distance apart. I called him uncle. He had a general store at Parippally Junction. My Chettayi had been a salesman there before he went abroad. After the day's business, Chettayi and Uncle came at around nine at night in their old Kinetic Honda scooter. He took his supper from Uncle's house and slept in the outhouse there. In most days, I would be alone in my house. My Chettayi was a trustee of my uncle's, so I used to call him Uncle's soul-keeper. In Uncle's absence, he would be the cashier of the shop. A Kochannan was also there as a salesman to assist with the distribution of commodities to the buyers.

Occasionally, my Chettayi showed his responsibility as an elder brother. One day he told me to come to the shop. He did not say why I was called. After Plus Two schooling, a two-year education break was there in my life. I could not join any course because of the lack of financial aid. He called me after he had found a part-time job for me. I decided to do it after the compulsion of my uncle. The job was the distribution of morning newspaper. The newspaper's agent, Krishna Prasad, was too tired to cycle the entire route around the village area, and so he decided to recruit a subagent. Through my uncle, Chettayi chose the job for me because I too had a belly.

At the shop, my uncle introduced me to Krishna Prasad. He gave me one bicycle of his own and asked me to be at Parippally Junction at five in the morning for newspaper distribution training. I accepted the offer because I too needed some money to proceed in my studies. The training started on the next day. At five in the morning, I cycled to Parippally Junction and reached the veranda of the shop where newspaper agents set their newsprints in order. On the very first day, he had some notices from the Lions Club of the area, informing the general public about their annual day celebrations. Krishna Prasad told me to put the notice in every newspaper's inner pages for distribution along with it. In the beginning, I thought he did the work for charity, but when I finished, he gave me fifty rupees, saying, 'Thousand notices for 200 rupees—50 yours, and the rest mine.'

With a smile, I accepted the money.

For the first two days, I followed him to identify the houses and the brand of newspapers to be distributed to each one. On the third day, he followed me to watch whether I was distributing the daily to the right subscriber or not. I had to distribute three brands of newspapers—namely, *Kerala Kaumudi*, *Malayala Manorama*, and *The Hindu*. The Malayalam dailies were thrown into the subscribers' compounds while riding on the bicycle itself, whereas at the houses I had to distribute the English newspapers, I did it with so care. I had a special respect for the language and those who spoke it. I showed the same admiration in the matter of newspapers and their readers too. He gave me a one-kilometre highway area, and the rest were five kilometres in the subroutes. Covering the high-traffic highway area was very risky because the houses were situated on either side of the road. Krishna Prasad told me to distribute on one side first and come back to the next side since crossing from one side to the other would be risky. I followed suit. It took nearly one and half hours to finish the entire cycling. After that, I was free. First, I did the job with reluctance and then with happiness as I began to get the money.

I used to get 1,500 rupees per month for this work and sometimes with the tips for notice distribution. That was the first achievement in my life. With my first wage, I bought a cotton sari for my mother. It was a moment of pride for me and my mother. When I gave her the sari, she shed a few drops of tears on my head as she hugged me for what I did—even though she was a little disappointed because her wish was to make me a government employee.

All these past moments flashed in my mind. These were the frozen moments of my life's course.

I still remembered the day my fortune in life took a U-turn. It was a Sunday morning. The day's work started a little late, so till seven in the morning, I was engaged in the distribution of newspapers. One of the houses where I dropped a newspaper was the house of my former tuition teacher and principal of the Excellent Tutorial College, Sir Baiju. He was at his gate, waiting for the newspaper. Seeing me, he invited me to his house and asked about my studies. I told him that after my Plus Two education, I discontinued my studies due to the lack of financial help for higher studies.

Two years before, he had taught me English in the twelfth class. He knew well that I was so interested in the English language. I always remained top in his class for English test papers. He also knew that I had only one parent and so had excused several months of fees for me in his institute. He allowed me to continue only because of my merit in my studies. I fulfilled his wish by remaining the topper of the batch in the English subject. Among the science students, I had performed well in the English language. My photo was also tagged in his results notice of the year as I remained the highest scorer in the English language from his institute.

He was not pleased to see me in the newspaper boy's attire.

He asked me, 'Are you willing to teach?'

'Where, sir?'

'In my tutorial. You are going to teach English for the fifth- to seventh-class students. Come tomorrow at seven thirty in the morning.'

He invited me to his tutorial to teach English for the lower classes. Thus, I began my second career as a tuition teacher after a two-year break in my education. Teaching the tuition students in the upper primary classes was my first assigned duty in the tutorial. That regenerated my taste in studying. Then I began to write a new page in my life. Consequently, I decided to renew my once-wound-up education.

The first time I heard the address of 'sir', that generated a moment of pride and self-respect in my life. My tastes began to change immediately. I began to read classical magazines, like *India Today*, *Mathrubhumi Weekly*, *Kalakaumudi*, *Bhashaposhini*, etc. I began an effort to show my intellectual tastes to other senior teachers in the tutorial as well as among the students. The students took interest in my classes. Within two months, I got a promotion to teach in eighth and ninth classes. Being an English teaching staff member in a tutorial after passing just the twelfth class, I felt embarrassment, so I decided to continue my stopped study.

Sir Baiju told me to stop the menial work of newspaper distribution in the early morning and to engage in my studies further. But I did not think it was a menial work as it served as my support in life. I remembered one of the Malayalam teachers who did two works—teaching in tutorials and collecting coconuts for sale from his own students' houses. He never felt any shame in it. After all, I thought, I was not a regular government employee to consider other works as menial. Everyone knew that what we get from tuition was not enough to meet all our basic needs.

But I felt the essence of Sir Baiju's remark in a later day. While I was throwing the newspaper to the house of one of my students, she was astonished to see me and called out, 'Hi, our English teacher.' She told her classmates, 'Sir Nilesh is our newspaper boy.' The next day as I entered the class, the entire division began to chuckle.

'What happened? Why are you laughing?' I asked them.

One little boy in the front row pointed to the blackboard. I turned to the board and saw the drawing of a newspaper boy on his bicycle. Someone drew a newspaper boy's caricature on the blackboard with the comment 'English newspaper boy'. I joined with them in laughter. The chuckle turned into a high-sounding laugh. I never asked who drew the caricature.

I just wished him a good future in art. Then slowly I began to explain seriously that every job had its own status. I told them that I was not like them. I had no mother or father, so I had to work hard to support myself. They listened to me quietly, and most of them became regretful. The girl who saw me distributing the newspapers told me 'Sorry' and began to suffer regret for me; a kind of devotion began to grow in her little heart. I wiped it away from her mind, considering her as only a little kid.

In the summer vacation, I spent more time in the tuition centre. The classes were up to one o'clock in the afternoon. The purpose of summer vacation classes was to cover the entire syllabus before the school opened for the coming academic year.

After a few months' experience in teaching, I began to get offers to teach up to the tenth-class students of the neighbourhood's tuition centres. But I simply refused and joined my degree course through distance education. After my registration in the course, I joined a parallel college at Kollam. As I began to go for my studies, I did not get enough time to do the work of a newspaper boy. Several days I had to plead with Krishna Prasad for my inability to do the job.

I could follow these two careers only for a short period for the reason of time scarcity. One was in the early morning as a newspaper boy distributing dailies and periodicals to about 250 houses, including my previous tuition teacher. And in the late morning, I had to take tuition classes for the high school students of Excellent Tutorial. So I dropped the job of a newspaper boy.

Three years flew away, with the ease of a fresh breeze. My days were made with teaching, studying, and socializing with people. During these years, I learnt the value of education, money, and relations. The greatest ever loss in my life also happened during this period, and that was the death of my mother, my only companion at home and my relentless source of love, care, and food.

The new twist in my life gave me a lot of diverse thoughts. The turn towards romance gave me a lot of reasons to revise my life. The girl I met here in my new class shook the romantic chamber of my heart, which had been till then an empty place. I became a regular observer of her. Later, the observation turned into devotion and love, a kind of heart-rending love that only a true lover could understand.

She used to sit on the right window seat where the western wind would come and chat with her locks. Seeing the dancing locks on her cheeks, an array of romantic huts pushed open in my heart which told me to rob her. It enticed me to create an opportunity to mingle with her without her being aware. We engaged in friendly talks during free times. I opened my life to her as innocently as possible. One day she told me she was called by the pet name Ammini Kuppi in her household. I thought it was a name that contains love, tenderness, and affection. Her dad and mum would call her by this name. She had a younger sister named Kavu, who was a twelfth-class student in a public school at her village. Little by little, she started sharing her familial life with me after nine to ten months of acquaintance.

It was a cloudy Wednesday during the tea break recess at eleven thirty. Shalini mounted the lecture dais and announced, 'Today we will have a celebration during the lunch break. It is nothing but the cutting of the birthday cake of our sweet Fatima Basir . . .' Her sweet voice echoed in the lecture hall.

I said, 'So we can expect a grand treat today. Yah.'

'That Fatima has to reply,' said Shalini.

'Bilkul . . . mei aap keliye treat karoongi . . .' Fatima replied in her mother's mother tongue. She was from Barmer, a Pakistan border district of Rajasthan. Her father was a Mallu. Years ago he went there to join the Indian Army. But his destiny was to turn into a travel agent and become a zamindar, a landlord there. He married a Rajasthani Muslim woman and settled there. He sent his daughter to his parents' house to learn his own family's and land's culture, and thus she became our classmate.

After the second hour, Nimmy requested me to bring the cake and snacks from the Lakshmi bakery at the college junction to celebrate the birthday. I agreed with pleasure. I took Apsy with me, and we bunked the slot for phonetics and rode to College House. Before we had our lunch at College House Restaurant, we went to Lakshmi Cookies and ordered for a two-kilogram Black Forest birthday cake, a musical flower candle, and three packets of fancy balloons to be parcelled. Before packing the cake, the baker asked us what name was to be emblazoned on the cake. On a slip, we wrote the words 'Happy Twentieth birthday to Fatima'.

After the meal, we brought the parcel into the class and decorated the dais and board with the balloons. Nimmy and I went to the coordinator's room to welcome her for the function. She used to take the first session after lunch so she was our chief guest for the celebration. For me, it was an opportunity to show my event management skill to Nimmy and an opportunity to mingle with her. I realized that the events of celebrations bring hearts together. I felt a step closer to Nimmy after the birthday celebration of Fatima. I really wished for the return of such celebrations. At least, such functions provided us with the opportunity of sharing responsibilities. It was a joyful thing to share the responsibility with the one I loved most. I prayed only for that.

A girl is like a piece of clay. It takes any shape that the artist wishes to give it. It has no definite shape or undeviating rigidity. Its shape and rigidity depends on the hands of the man who gives shape to it. If you are a real artist, you can make her a beloved one. She will be ready to love you to any extent. The mind of a girl takes its shape in the artistic hands of the man near to her. You can create a replica of your desired mind in her. The only thing you need is the creativity of man's woman-making skill. Before real men, all women are girls only.

My friends often used to say that I had the skill of woman-making.

CHAPTER 6

The ambience of the college was severely affected by the state politics. It naturally affected more those who were directly involved in the campus politics than those who were indirectly involved in it. Politics is a ruse. If you don't know the high tricks of the game, you will be defeated easily. It is the only game where you have to face opposition from inside your team and the opponent's. Being truthful to love is comprehensible, but being truthful to politics is something idiotic, my personal experiences taught me.

The motive behind keeping the PG classes on the third floor was to avoid the noisy scenes of campus politics. The college having the maximum batches of under graduation, post graduation and research wings among the affiliated colleges under University of Kerala is in fact like a mini university centre. The college is also notorious for political clashes and murdering. Those who lost their lives in the violent clashes were made martyrs in the party list.

A month before the second semester exam began, the unit secretary of SFI called me. He invited me for an agitation in front of Kollam Collectorate to protest against the solar scandal even though the real reason remained the Congress government's approval for the CBI probe into the larger-conspiracy angle in the TP murder case. TP was a revolutionary communist leader who was hacked to death in broad daylight by the paid assassins of his rival political group, the CPI(M).

TP had started his political career as an SFI activist and even represented SFI in the national level and dedicated his life for the party. When he was expelled from the same party, he was forced to form a splinter communist party called Revolutionary Marxist Party. He proved his leadership quality by winning the Onchiyam local polls. That aggravated the CPI(M). The former cadre was written off as a victim of political feud by CPI(M).

He had been a supporter of the VS fraction of CPI(M). His expulsion and formation of a splinter group cost a loss to the party. They had lost their permanent Lok Sabha seat of Vadakara where the slain leader had been a candidate. Kerala Marxists were more devoted to their party than to any other relations. They did not allow any tree to come over the roof even if it could produce money. If it did, they would cut it. They followed this policy in TP's case also.

The CPI(M) charged him with the accusation of splitting the CPI(M) workers and forming a rival group. Taking this indictment in consideration, the party's district and state level committees took a bloody decision to behead the chief of the split group. The second gaffe they did was they gave the bloody mission to a 'quotation' gang (paid killers) and named the mission as Kannur Model. The cadre was murdered on a public road with fifty-one dagger taunts, most of which were on his face. It was a brutal slaughter which affected the conscience of the entire state.

The agitators had no right to protest against the government's present decision of forwarding the case to CBI, the nation's prime investigators. Yet they had to dissent against the government, divert the attention of the media and the general public, and threaten the ruling government. The solar scandal was a good weapon for the opposition to harness against the ruling front. The scandal was mixed up with a mass involvement of sexual exploitation of the masterminds behind the scandal which included several influential members of the ruling party. So CPI(M) considered it as a good weapon to conceal the TP murder case. It was a political gimmick, which all parties used to play to escape from the public's attention.

The government made the decision of allowing a CBI probe after a hunger strike in front of the Secretariat led by the widow of the victim and supporters of the Revolutionary Marxist Party. They also got the prop up of the veteran communist VS, who wrote a letter to the chief minister regarding the murder and the necessity of an enquiry. Even the party 'considers the letter written by comrade V. S. Achuthanandan, as leader of the opposition, to the chief minister of Kerala, as a wrong step and not in conformity with the stand of the party'. It forced the party to constitute a party-level enquiry committee and probe the case. The high-level party enquiry team found out about the fact of personal rivalry between TP and a local committee member being the cause of the murder, and the accused was expelled from the party's primary membership. But the probe was not enough to appease the public's conscience.

Even the veteran communist VS finally agreed with the party probe. He decided finally that the party was bigger than any other sentiment, person, and even truth. He proved himself a party stalwart by doing a volte-face from his previous stand as he realized the soil erosion from under his own party, which pained him. He was always more loyal to his party than even to his own wife. That was why even Karat, the all-India general secretary of CPI(M), respects him. He often tried to correct the wrong path of his party workers to maintain public support for his party.

To protest against the new decision of the government, the CPI(M) decided to conduct a district-level agitation demanding the resignation of Chief Minister Oommen Chandy, whose office was involved in the solar scandal. The CPI(M) and its youth wing, DYFI, had already started their protest. Now the student wing of the party was also instructed to do so. So I was called from the class to form the front row of the protest. Usually, I was not called for such agitations and protests of party politics. But this time they compelled me to take part in it. I told the chairman that I was a supporter of the VS fraction of the party and asked why I had to come. Further, I explained my stand that VS's volte-face was only to protect the party because he knew he was the endorsement of CPI(M) in Kerala. But even now he was against the murder, and his U-turn was not the fifty-second chop on TP but a pat on his own party.

The chairman suggested me, 'For a future in politics, we have to follow the official wing of the party and not any ideology, especially a party like ours where no individual is above the organization.'

I did not want to build any political future, but I wanted to establish a good relation while in college, so I agreed to follow them.

As the protest march reached the Kollam District Collectorate, the protesters were barricaded by the police. We shouted slogans louder than before.

'Oommen Chandy moorachy, rajivekku purathupoku.' Step down, Chief Minister.

'Sarithorjam! Sarithorjam! Oommen Chandy manthrisabhakku sarithorjam.' Oommen Chandy ministry under the spell of Saritha sun power energy.

As per the instructions, we began to break the barricades. Some of us, even I did not know who they were, began pelting stones at the police force. The district police superintendent ordered for a lathi charge against the agitators. Before I could do anything, a stroke fell on my forehead, and I collapsed on the road. Somebody took me and put me in a vehicle, and I was admitted in the district hospital of Kollam.

In the evening, from AKG Centre, the official headquarters of the Marxist Communist Party of India in the Kerala zone, comrade Sreemati teacher visited the hospital for an enquiry into the severity of the police attack. Along with me, three others were also admitted. I didn't know who they were, but they had participated in the agitation for their personal gains. No other prominent student leaders got injured in the attack. Later I came to know that these leaders were acquaintances of the police force. So they targeted only the strange faces there. They knew that these strange faces were political coolies. They took me also in the coolie group.

When my classmates came to visit me on the next day, Nimmy asked me, 'How do you feel now?'

I answered, 'Fine.'

'Who is looking after you?'

'Elder cousin,' I replied.

Kuttathichechi, my uncle's elder daughter, would spend the daytime with me. After sending her children to school, she would come to me. During the night, Uncle sent Thavadi Rajan, a boy in my village, to look after me at the hospital.

Then Robin asked, 'When will you be discharged from the hospital?'

'Most probably tomorrow itself.'

On the three days I spent in the district hospital, I was like an arising comrade in the realm of Kerala politics.

When everyone united, the pressure mounted on the ruling government, and they in a roundabout way forced CBI to reject the case. The party cadres celebrated the decision with bursting firecrackers. Sometimes the high-ranking chairs of a party are made of blood and sins.

The communist party should follow the *adavunayam*, the secret agenda and secret alliance, to face hurdles. The cadre party could follow all the secret political alliances to keep away the opponents, especially the national front NDA, from winning a seat in Kerala. Even at the time when the thirty-year-old Indian political record was rewritten by Modi by winning in the 16th Lok Sabha election, with BJP reigning over majority of the seats, the communists didn't allow the lotus to blossom in the state. They succeeded in their stand to overcome the Narendra Modi wave that had flown all over India. That wave could not make any effect in Kerala, but it made a triangular contest in the Thiruvananthapuram constituency.

After the incident, when I went to the college, my friends came to my class and enquired after my health. My department head also enquired after my health, and that gave me great solace. Usually, teachers never asked anything related with campus politics or its turnouts. They were not supporters of it. So I felt it like my own mother was asking me about my health.

I learnt a lesson in life and politics from the hospital bed. When I was ill, I was all alone and had to even pay for a bystander. Politics always needs prey, and the unproven guys like me would be victimized by it.

The rest of the month was busy with exams and preparations. Nimmy and I shared as usual all the study materials we had except our hearts.

CHAPTER 7

The second semester exam was over. Third semester started without any gap. I felt no progress in my love affair. She still listed me only in her friends circle. I doubted whether there was such an object as a love-generating object in humans.

The research scholars used to visit their guides and sometimes conducted seminars, workshops, and paper presentations in the seminar hall of the college. For all such functions, we were regular invitees. We served as the patient audience. Once, a French social worker visited our college to present a paper entitled 'The Suicidal Tendency of Keralites'. She was asked a remedy for the menace of family suicides that involved innocent children; before budding, these children had to surrender their lives to their own parents.

'Why do they take their own children with them? Is it because of the feeling of insecurity they have about their children, like who would be there to look after the children?'

She had to face a series of questions from the audience. She tried to reply in a manner that said she wanted to analyze the root cause of this tendency. 'The prompts for suicide were financial instability and false pride on values, status quo, money, and man–woman relations. To find a solution to the root causes of these prompts of suicidal tendency can solve the problem.' This was her observation. 'There was not a solid solution for it,' she continued, 'yet the circumstances in the family, both internal and sometimes external issues, might cause the destruction of a family. We have to avoid such situations in our lives. A parental consideration from the government like that of parents to their children can help to mitigate the grave situation. Police stations with counselling services should be opened in such areas.'

In such seminars and in out-of-the-classroom programmes, Nimmy and I would share adjacent seats. She began to consider me as a member of her own family. I saw that attachment was growing in her. With every drop of a calendar page, my relationship with her takes a step up of her friendship ladder. Could it be that the end of friendship is love?

Halfway of the third semester, we got an opportunity to go to English and Foreign Languages University, Hyderabad, for collecting study materials for the rest of the semester. Professor Meera gave us the permission to go to EFLU in Hyderabad after the recommendation of Professor Harris, who was dealing with twentieth-century literature.

Professor Meera was a widow. Her husband had died in a road accident after sharing four years of their marital life. Sometimes she showed her contempt on ruling parties for the poor maintenance and low capacity of roads. Every year, Kerala would lose people in road accidents, which would be more than the loss of lives in a major war between two countries. There are no parallel improvements of road capacity with the increase of vehicle population. It made many road accident victims every year. Human life has only the worth of a street dog on roads.

When her husband died, she had been waiting for her second child. She had been seven months pregnant at the time of his death. His death shocked her a lot, and her child, born later, was a victim of the mishap. Even at the age of 17, the child remained unhealthy. Her loyalty to her husband was an unending one. She never married again. The male students of the college worshipped her as a role model for girls.

I thought on several occasions, 'Did she love him that much?'

She remained a living example of true love in life. She was such a frank and innocent lady, but an unlucky heir of many a road accident victims in the state.

She sanctioned us to go for a library trip to the central university in Hyderabad. She treated everyone with confidence and showed loyalty to all humans. Suspicion was not a word in her personal dictionary; she believed in each and every soul.

In advance, we booked e-tickets for the journey for an entire room in the B1 coach of Sabari Express. We scheduled our trip on 15 October and the return journey on the 25th, the pooja day, on the same train. Except for Reshmi, the entire group was ready to go to Hyderabad; Reshmi had her elder brother's engagement on the date, so she was left out from the trip. But we did not cancel her already booked ticket till the day before our journey.

On the day of the journey, we gathered at the Kollam Railway Station platform no. 5. We were thrilled about the journey. Nobody was there to accompany us as our escort. We men took special care of our counterparts and their luggage. Not more than half an hour of waiting there, we heard the announcement for our train.

'Passengers, your kind attention please. Train no. 17229 from Trivandrum Central to Hyderabad is coming on to platform no. 5.' Then the same matter was announced in

Hindi and Malayalam. The sharp female voice alerted the passengers there. After the announcement, we waited for five minutes for the train to reach the platform. As we saw the train approaching, we readied ourselves with the backpacks and the handbags. We were comfortably housed in our cabin. Our study trip to India's biggest academic library was begun in a joyful mood. A thirty-hour journey to our destination started at eight twenty in the Indian railway time.

Travelling together makes people more intimate. Even strangers behave more amicably during long travels. The mind needs a secure feeling when we go away from our domain. We try to get that security from our fellow passengers. The same feeling was generated in our minds also.

It was the idea of Professor Harris, who advised us to go to EFLU in Hyderabad for material collection and confirmation of the project topic for the last semester. He gave us an introductory letter to the programme coordinator of MA in English Literature, Professor Julu Zen. She was professionally and personally a friend of Professor Harrison; they had worked together for four years in the University of Calcutta.

The journey meant much more to me than the purpose of studying. It gives a change for my friendship with Nimmy to deepen even more. It was my first trip out of the state. It was completely an escortless journey; no faculty member or parent was accompanying us. We had pre-planned to come alone to the railway station from home, which was not far away from our college but just a 15-minute leisure walk.

For the first few hours, our mobile cameras flashed hither and thither. Everyone was eager to capture the moments of happiness. When the train reached the Kayamkulam Railway Station, the ticket examiner came. I showed my mobile message from IRCTC, and he asked me to pronounce the PNR number. I did so, and later he claimed an ID proof from one of us. I showed my college ID. He took it and looked the details in it. With approval on his face, he moved to the adjacent cabin.

We resumed our talk.

I was the only one in the flock who came with my personal belongings only; the other seven in the band crammed their backpacks with edible items for the entire odyssey. Just after one hour of the journey, we took our breakfast of idlis, dosas, coconut chutney, and sambar. As assigned, every one brought their own share, and my contributions were the disposable plates and glasses. Nimmy brought special sambar, and Reshmi brought coconut chutney. Robin's contribution was the bananas that were cultivated in his own field.

'Wow! What a tasty saaambaaaar! Who made it, Nimmy, your amma?' I lavished her with phrases of praise.

She said, 'Yes, my mummy's special. She never uses brinjals in sambar. According to her, brinjals gave a dark look to the curry.'

'That's good,' I replied.

All of a sudden, Apsy remarked, 'Aliya, appam thinnal pore, kuzhi ennano?' Brother-in-law, just eat the Appam, don't count the moulds. It meant that I should just enjoy the final product and not worry about where it originated.

He was such a tactless character who often made unnecessary comments on pious occasions like this. He could not have a low-pitch speaking voice. When he spoke, he was audible to the whole neighbourhood. One day, the four of us—Nimmy, Seemol, Reshmi, and I—were in the kiosk to have our evening snacks and tea. We were chatting about some personal matters. The topic of our discussion was Seemol's marriage proposal. She said she had a proposal from an MBBS doctor. She told this to us in a very controlled voice so only our peer group would hear.

But all of a sudden, Apsy remarked, 'A doctor would never marry her as she is only a literature student, and beyond that, it would not be an equal-rank marriage.'

His voice attracted the attention of the other people present there. They began to notice our group. Nimmy gestured for him to lower his voice. But he gave no heed to her request. Immediately, I switched over to another topic of discussion. He couldn't understand why I changed the topic all of a sudden, but the girls in the gang immediately picked up the new topic of the oncoming visiting professor for our class.

He was such a typical character; therefore, I felt no shame in his present comment. He was frank in his comments. What he felt, he spoke it out freely. I simply laughed it away.

Anyhow, it was a sumptuous breakfast for all of us. We really enjoyed the company and the sharing of responsibilities than the food we had. The food had the touch of companionship in it.

The post-breakfast discussion was on study matters and critical books. Shilpa tried to explain the contents of *Wasteland*. It was really a good attempt to share the contents and imprint them in our minds. The discussion on a new contest attracted all of us. The dramatization of the dialogues in it really created in us a thorough picture of the poem even though it contained some funny characteristics. It is human tendency to get a better understanding of difficult texts.

At about twelve thirty, the pantry server started his distribution of packed midday meals to those who had already ordered for it. It stimulated our appetite also. We also opened our meal containers and had our lunch. It was really a buffet session of homemade meals with Fatima's special chicken roast. After the meal, all of us took a short nap, which was truly imposed on us by our co-passengers because we realized that our noisy cabin might disturb their sleep.

'Coffee, hot coffee,' the call of a coffee vendor woke us up again at around three in the afternoon.

I ordered coffee for the entire party. We were recharged fully for the next round of chatting and then a music session. We did not know that Fatima was such a good singer.

Shilpa wanted a song from Fatima. We encouraged her to sing. She accepted our request and began to sing a Hindi film song. 'Jeene legaa hoon pehley se zyaadaa, pahley se zyaadaa tumpey marney lagaa hun.' She sang in a beautiful tone that really excited all of us. The song touched my heart. I really felt like she sang the song for me.

In the evening, the train reached the holy place of Tirupati. A lot of rail passengers on the platform ran with their luggage, pots, offerings to god, and some with their little children to find a place somewhere on the train. Most of these devotees had shaven heads without the differentiation of gender or age. Beyond the passengers trying to get into our train, a big crowd of devotees was waiting for other trains to come into the station.

As the train just moved from the station, a havoc was heard from the adjacent bogie; a woman jumped out of it, causing minor injury to her limbs. As the train had already started, the woman panicked because her husband and child hadn't entered the train. She had a handbag of some foods with her. She threw it on to the platform, and the next moment, she jumped out of the moving train. She fell on the platform; luckily, she didn't lose her life, getting only minor injuries. Watching the panic in the platform, the rail guard waved his red flag, and the train came to a halt again in the same station.

Nimmy and I were at the door to see where the Tirupati temple was, but we could not see the temple. We only saw the accident. The railway police personnel and two TTRs rushed to the spot where the incident had happened. After a short enquiry, they registered a case against the woman who had jumped out of a running train. We were relieved ourselves, for no danger had happened to her other than the petty case the railway police registered against her.

Meanwhile, a vendor of jasmine, a teenage girl, came before us. She had a basket in her hand which was filled with jasmine garlands of white and sunglow. She put it down in front of us. She put forward a cord of the garland to Nimmy, hoping that she would be a sure buyer for her. Women are so fond of flowers. Nimmy too showed her love towards flowers. The fragrance of the flowers made the place an Eden of romance. First she refused to buy it, but the girl forced her to take it.

'Pachas rupiye dedo faiyya . . .' The girl then demanded money from me, thinking that her client was someone dear to me.

'Ithane fool ko ithani paise naheem de sakthihoom.' Nimmy refreshed her spoken Hindi only for the sake of bargain.

'Aur doongi deedi, chinda mat kijiye, ye painkar aap aur sunder benti hei . . . aur aap ki dil meeta hojayengi.' The teenager promoted her sale.

As Nimmy had no purse with her except for the god-made purse which was preserved for me, at the spot, I got an opportunity to pay for her. Thus, the first thing I bought for her was the garland of jasmine. A rare gift for a not-yet-recognized love affair. As I gave the girl money, the train set out for its next destination.

In our cabin, the womenfolk divided the garland among themselves. Some kept it on hand, and some on their hair.

'Giving a garland to a monkey,' Apsy's comment made Shilpa laugh a lot.

Nimmy tried to pin it on her silky hair, but it did not stay there. Seemol took it from her and fixed it to her hair. Nimmy pulled the entire hair over her right shoulder. She looked so enchanting in her new look. I was stunned by her beauty with the flower cord.

At 9 p.m., our neighbours were preparing their berths for sleep. I thought that these people travel in trains to get their full stretch of sleep. They were not disturbed by housework and TV shows inside the train. They really took full rest during the journey. It seemed like this was the first time they had a break day in the entire year of busy work. One by one, the passengers in every cabin in the coach went to sleep. We too occupied our berths after wishing good night to each other. The rest of the chats were made from our berths that we occupied. Till around eleven, it continued.

We woke up a little late the next morning. The female group woke up and refreshed themselves before we did. We were woken up by them at around nine in the morning. After a quick brushing and toileting, we geared up ourselves for a breakfast of bread and omelette.

That day, our discussion began with the incident at the Tirupati Railway Station the day before; it was an open discussion for all of us.

'Why did the woman jump out of the moving train as she could alight at the next station and inform her husband that she was waiting for him there?' I introduced the topic.

Shilpa argued, 'The woman was panic-stricken as she found her family was not with her.'

'It was sheer ignorance on the woman's side on what to do and how to do it,' Robin said.

'She might not have money with her or a mobile to contact her husband,' Apsy speculated.

'Perhaps she could not bear the separation from her family,' opined Nimmy. She used to think everything related to familial background.

'Maybe she was travelling for the first time in a train and could not know where to alight and how to deal with the situation,' Seemol told us her opinion.

Thus, the discussion went on for half an hour. This and more topics we conversed about till the train reached Secunderabad Railway Station.

We reached our destination at around one thirty in the afternoon. The entire journey was as thrilling as a Bollywood super movie. Robin came with a list of the attractions in Hyderabad and the navigation route map of CEFL from Secunderabad in his pamphlet. After alighting at the Secunderabad Junction, we hired two auto rickshaws to take us to CEFL.

CHAPTER 8

A labyrinth of a campus welcomed us. We couldn't make out which road led to the academic building. The signboards showed the routes, but they were confusing ones. We asked the people we met on the way to the campus to find the location of Professor Julu Zen's official room. Finally, we reached her department room. But it was closed. Somebody suggested us to go to her residence. So we left the academic building and moved towards the residential area of the university campus. On the first floor of the four-quarter building, we finally met her. A fat and round woman in her fifties with an English accent opened the door. She welcomed us to her quarters. Professor Harris had already phoned her, and she was expecting us. Shalini gave her the recommendation letter from our college. She arranged for the facilities for our temporary stay in the university guest hostels. We decided to collect all the necessary study materials from the vast library after choosing the enlisted books of reference. The library provided us with the facility for economically photocopying entire books of our choice.

The CEFL campus was a mini India in the sense that you would get a sample of people from every state of India. From Kashmirians to Tamilians, different people would come here to learn different foreign languages. For me, the campus was a wonder packed in letters. Everyone got freedom in the campus. You could see several Radha–Krishna couples here. It was part of a feminist movement in the campus to give a man a womanish look and make him live in the women's hostel. The pair would be known as a Radha–Krishna couple. They would have the freedom to do anything between them. It was a kind of pre-marital coupling life to enjoy the body. Women had a secret agenda behind this; they never wanted to care for their body as it was a female body. They wanted to generate the unnatural tendencies in them by showing unwanted trends and shedding the natural shyness. Whatever body parts they have, they wanted to expose them and wanted to do whatever things men sought to do. They wanted equality of rights in their life too by the way of blindly imitating the world of men. An onlooker might doubt whether it was equality of rights or equality of doing vulgarity in life. Whatever it was, they enjoyed doing it.

The campus gave us several cultural shocks. The sight of promising teenage girls of India with lighted cigarettes in their reddish lips was one of them. During every recess, most of these young Indian females would smoke in the campus publicly, just in front of their teachers. Even though the campus was declared a smoking-free area, these rules were not meant for the new generation of womenfolk here.

We preferred to spend most of our time in the library, choosing books of our demand. On the third day of our visit, Nimmy and I went to the dissertation room of the library. A large collection of dissertations were kept in large rows of racks. We searched for an ideal pattern of research work to take photos of them with our mobile CamScanner in order to get guidelines for our dissertation work for the final semester. Our search landed us at one of the last rows of the big hall.

To our surprise, we saw two lovers deeply engaged in lip-lock kissing in this vacant part of the library. As they saw us, they told us to go to the next row. They thought we too went there to do the same. Nimmy immediately looked at my eyes, and she winked at me to come away from there.

In the evening, we went to see the famous historical monument Charminar. Nimmy was so afraid to climb the narrow circular staircase leading to the upper storey of the plague memorial. She held on to my arm just like a climbing grape vine to its supporter. I carried her like she was my own eyeball. The historical construction gave me something unforgettable in my life. First was its historic beauty, and second, I began to feel that a new history had begun in my life. I really thought a thing of 1591 triggered the love in her. The entire group thought Nimmy had fallen in love with me. Even I felt she really had begun to love me. But once she came down from the monument, she became as normal as ever. She forgot everything. Even the hug she had given me at a time when she had slipped on one of her steps. She forgot every touch of her body with mine. But I could not—simply because I loved her as my own life.

From there, we took a visit to the Hyderabadi pearl shops to purchase something for the female band. Then even on our journey back, I was not fully awakened from the hold of Nimmy.

She had begun to consider me as someone dear to her heart, I thought.

We met some Mallu students there. The Keralites outside Kerala is known by the name of Mallu. They welcomed us for the Friday dance in the academic block at midnight. Robin, Apsy, and I went to see it at twelve midnight. Almost all the male and female scholars assembled in the portico of the ground floor. Loudspeakers were kept on the four corners of the portico, and 'item' songs in Hindi and English were being played for the dance. Anyone in the campus could join in the dance programme. Mostly they performed in pairs of male and female. Most of the steps were enactments of sexual postures. They engaged in the act for energy release for their youthful bodies. The campus holidays for Saturday and Sunday were begun on the night of Friday itself. Our Mallu friends invited us to participate. But being strangers, we could not. Some of the pairs were drunk too.

After an hour or two, we asked our friends when the programme would come to an end. We got the reply: 'The programme will last till four o'clock in the morning.' So we left there sneakily.

The next morning, we went to our female group's hostel. It was a call away from ours. It was a surprise visit to their dormitory. As they saw us, Seemol instantly began to pick up the panties and brassieres from the window and chair tops.

'Why didn't you inform us about your visit?' While doing it, she criticized us.

'If so, how could we see it?' Robin retorted funnily.

Seemol knew Robin's weakness of stalking girls whose panty shapes were visible through their sari or churidar. For him, it was a sexier attraction than seeing a nude girl in front of him.

'I know you,' Seemol commented.

'What do you know?'

'Nothing.'

Nimmy and Shilpa interrupted their talk as they came from the bathroom after their shower and in gorgeous red and yellow round churidars. I looked at Nimmy. She passed a gentle smile at me. My apprehension flew away with her smile. Until that time, I was apprehensive of whether they would like our surprise visit to their dormitory or not. Anyhow, her smile gave me confidence to proceed there. We first gave the excuse to them that the reason of our visit was, as we were up earlier that day, we waited in front of the mess to have breakfast with them but then decided to go up to their hostel.

We shared our experience of the previous night at the Friday dance with our colleagues. Later, we went together for the mess. After a light breakfast of upma and tea, we simply engaged in our work. A lot of books were already photocopied to take back home.

We heard about the media room of the university where visual and audio study materials were produced for the school and college students. With our request, Dr Julu Zen took us into the media room of the university. She introduced us to the professor in charge of the media room, Mr Upendran. He shared a few minutes with us and told us the importance of using media, especially visual media, in the process of teaching. We saw a lot of e-materials for the school and college students being produced there.

A day before our return journey, we went to visit the famous Ramoji Film City. This journey also helped me to strengthen up our tie up of friendship. The site where the hit Malayalam film *Udayananu Tharam* was shot was interesting to all of us. We saw the replicas of India's most famous monuments there for the purpose of film-shooting. The huge structure of Taj Mahal, the living pictogram of never-ending love, created a sensational cry from Nimmy. It proved to me that she was not against love. After the day's expedition, we came back at eight in the evening.

I saw a utopian world in the campus. We were free to do anything there. The campus was an isolated island in the middle of the conventional land of Secunderabad. A mass of intellectual scholars lived there without any restrictions from the outside world. The teaching faculty of the university could not get involved in the life and activities of the so-called scholars. For us, the experience in the campus was something new and strange.

On the 25th, the pooja holiday, we left the campus at nine in the morning to board Sabari Express. On the return journey, we crammed our backpacks with the photocopies of study materials. In the afternoon of the next day, we reached Kollam station. As it was a Sunday, some of the parents came to the station to pick up their daughters. Nimmy's parents and her younger sister were also there to pick her up. We met one another and introduced ourselves.

The following week was a new beginning for us.

CHAPTER 9

Kerala is enchanting for three things—its flora, beaches, and girls. It is god's own country as well as it is girls' own country. The girls are given more importance in a home; so even their personal choices are taken collectively by the other members of the family, including father, mother, brothers and sisters young and old, uncles, and aunties—everyone has a responsibility in the 'she' matter.

It was a Saturday. After the class at Excellent Tutorial for the third-semester BA English students, I had my meal at Saji's Hotel at ESIC Junction and came back home. I didn't feel good. Some memories of my mother stirred in my heart. I sat back in my armchair and dozed off. I fell into a daydream in which I talked with my mother, who rarely comes to my dreams nowadays to comfort or console me. She had loved me so much; I could not know how mothers have that much deep affection for their children. I was the one so lucky with that. Even after her departure, she used to care for me, and she used to ease me in my troubles. As I dozed off, she came to pat my hair so lovingly. She knew well that I was all alone on this earth and that nobody was there to share my little home and big silence.

I woke up from my nap when my mobile rang.

The caller ID column was empty. I pressed the answer key to attend the call. It was a service provider call informing me about the special offer on the 3G data pack. I cancelled the call before hearing the offer. I logged in to my Facebook account. I just looked for any interesting post in it. There was no special message. Shalini had changed her profile picture on it. On the online link, I saw the green spot on Nimmy's profile. I opened the chat box for Ammini Kuppi.

'Hi . . . Nimmy, what r u doing, dr?'

She got my online chat and was now typing her reply.

'Hiiiiiiiiii . . . Nilesh.'

'First time I see u in the c/b.'

'Today I'm free. That's y.'

'Ok. What r u doing there?'

'I was just chatting with my ma.'

'How so?'

'Wireless messages. Direct from her heart to mine, without the support of any modern gadgets and the support of towers and handsets. A kind of telepathy . . .'

I felt so relieved to get someone so dear to convey this message to. I wanted to continue this chat for a good length of time. She typed her next message within a few seconds. It was easy to type with the laptop than the mobile handset.

The message box blinked with the words: 'Thu paagal hogaya kya?'

She was so fond of Hindi. She had spent some of her childhood years in Ahmedabad. So whenever she got an opportunity, she used to switch over to her dialect, Hindi. Furthermore, she was an ardent admirer of Hindi soaps in the TV channels, especially the soaps in the Colors Channel.

'U can't understand my mother. She is always . . . and always . . . with me.'

'Did she love u that much?'

'Still . . .'

'Nice . . . daaaa . . .'

'How goes ur studies there? Did u complete eighteenth-century literature?' I queried her.

'I'm not so intelligent like u. It takes time 4 me to complete an entire paper.'

'Wow! What a wonderful observation . . .' I mistook it for a joke.

The chat box showed she was typing.

'What?'

'Who is so intelligent, u or me?' I asked her.

'Without a doubt, u r d meritorious scholar in our batch.'

'But I always feel that u r d one,' I said her.

'B4 ur chat with ma what wr u doing there?'

'I just finished Shakespeare's *Romeo and Juliet*'

I wrote a white lie on my message box to create an opportunity to talk with her on the topic of love. But she did not realize it as I deliberately put the names Romeo and Juliet because it was also a prescribed text in our sixteenth-century English literature paper.

'How did u feel about it?' she asked me.

'*Fine*. An unmatchable love affair.'

'I had already read it in my BA class.'

'How did u feel about it then?'

'Just wndrfl!' After a pause, she sent me another message: '? 4u.' I have a question for you

'*s*.' My reply was a tiny smile.

'Y r u *s*?' she asked me.

'U can ask A3.' I gave her the permission to ask a question anytime, anywhere, and any place—the A3.

'Hv u ever got an LL [love letter]?'

'No, nvr. Who wil give me such a gud thing? . . . Why? Dd u get an LL from somebody?'

'No, nothing like that.'

'Then what? Tday, who wil write an LL? L is expressed directly.' I posted my reply.

'LL is smtg interesting.' She was in a mood to talk about love matters.

'Do you want an LL?'

'Majak math karo.' She switched on to her Hindi.

'I'm rdy 2 giv u sample LL.'

'4 what?'

'Just 4 fun. Just 4 u to know wht s LL.'

'Do you mean a replica of LL?'

'Yaaaaaaaaaaaah . . . a fake love letter, I'll consider u as my lover & write an LL.'

'Ok, I agree.'

'I will bring it the next day.'

The chatting took me to a point where I got the opportunity to craft a fake love letter.

'But it should be passionate & content-enriched one,' she frankly said to me without showing any emotional touch in it. Before I could complete my reply, her next message appeared on the box. 'C u. Ma calling . . .'

'Bye . . . bye . . .'

But she was no longer online to read my bye. Her mother had called her, and she posted a 'See you' message.

An unwavering mind couldn't be changed easily at any cost, especially one that is devoted to parents. So a hard task was before me to mould her mind towards me.

But after the chat, I felt I was on top of the world.

The turning point of our friendship came all of a sudden. On Sunday night, I started writing a love letter; it was not a fake one, but with the real feelings in my mind.

You are the poem of my life. You are falling like a soft shower and make my heart's barren land fertile. If you are not there, the roses would remain impotent in the barren land of my heart. You awaken the hidden seeds in the garden of my heart and make them sprout like the rain does to the land with drought. You give colour and aroma to the forsaken rose garden of my heart. You make it a garden of colours.

When I see you, these roses produce the fragrance of all the perfumes of Arabia. When I see you in my mind's eye, you produce the chilly mist of Kashmir. What are you made of, maiden? Love or beauty or simplicity? You are my heartbeat in every breath that I don't want to breathe it out. If you are there, seven springs come together. If you are there, I am the emperor of seven kingdoms. If you are there, I'm the lucky heir of all humanity. If you are there, I'm the god of love. I feel you are like the deer in a virgin forest. You bring the cool breeze into my garden. Won't you accept my deep-rooted love for you?

One request, tell the sun not to light, tell the moon not to shine, but don't tell me to forget you. Tell the roses not to spread fragrance and tell the clouds not to fly, but don't tell me to stop loving you. My heart is spilling with the nectar of words when I write about you. Will you give me your heart in return?

Lalsalam.

I ended the letter with an expression borrowed from the communist terminology of Malayalam, *lalsalam*, which is usually used by a leader as a leave-taking phrase after addressing the mass of comrades in a public meeting.

Could a woman ever forget the man who first undressed her to reveal that nude body of hers? I wanted to create such an effect in her mind with the opportunity before me.

On New Year's Day, when the college reopened after the Christmas break, I gave the letter to her by hand for her perusal of it.

'What is it?'

'You don't know?'

'Really, please . . . Da . . . Tell me, what is it?'

'Don't dramatize the situation. You asked me to write a fake love letter. I prepared one for you. Take it, and read it at home.' I gave it to her without the others noticing and gestured for her to keep it in her Diesel backpack.

But she unfolded it and began to read it as coolly as if it was a grocery bill. As she proceeded to read the piece of writing, I noticed the light in her eyes, which spoke louder than words. Her rosy cheeks blushed with blue blood that spread like a drop of ink in a glass of pure water.

'I need a reply.' I laughed. She blinked her eyes in such a manner as if she was considering me her newborn baby.

The next day, I was eagerly waiting for her arrival. I wound up my tuition class ten minutes early and reached the college a few minutes earlier than the regular time. Something was there in my mind that had begun to disturb my thoughts. That something told me to go earlier and feel the presence of the place where she and I share. I really began to feel lovesick, a feeling that only a lover could understand. But my waiting proved fruitless. She didn't turn up on that day. I sent a WhatsApp message of enquiry. 'Hey, where r u? Tell me please!'

The class had already started. I kept the cell in my hand so I would feel the message alert. Even after a long wait, no message received.

A little bit of apprehension arose in me. I didn't know why. That was the day I expected more, the day I received less, the day I felt the pang of love, true love, like that of the pang of a brook that has to separate its trunk of water into two smaller streams.

I asked Reshmi, 'Where is she?'

'Who?' she replied even though she knew whom I meant.

'Hey, Nimmy.'

'I don't know.'

'Didn't she call you?'

'No. Why do I have to call her if you are here?' She was making fun of me.

'Okayyyyyy, dear . . . I will manage it anyhow.'

It was the first time that I sensed that the whole class had smelled the fragrance of my heart in love. I wondered how they caught up with the changes in my inner thoughts; I really doubted whether it produced any scent from the rose garden of my own heart.

During break and lunchtime, I waited for her call or message. After lunch, Reshmi made a call to her landline number. It rang for some time and ended. Nobody was there to attend it.

The day felt like a year for me. I sensed an apprehension like that of a mother whose daughter was being proposed to by a good family and was waiting for the groom's reply.

I bunked the last hour of the day. I told Robin that I had a class at Kottiyam. I had evening tuition class from four to five for the BA fifth-semester students of NSS College of Kottiyam. I arrived there in advance time.

I took out the poetry book from the lockless shelf of College of English to refer to it once again. I had already scribbled all the references, difficult explanations, and even hints on situational jokes to be cracked in the class. A parallel college teacher had to entertain the students with the display of knowledge and with the timely cracking of jokes. Otherwise, he would be incompatible for the industry. The batch consisted of a pack of fifteen students of nine girls and six boys—all of them three or four years junior to me. For an onlooker, it was a difficult task to distinguish between the tutor and the students.

Last year, this was the same text I had studied for my final-year exam, and this year, I was teaching it to my students. For teaching, I had to prepare each and every phrase and references in the text. For this purpose, I utilized the university's centre library in our college campus and Internet browsing. The cost-free use of Internet and reference books helped me to compete in this field. In study matters, I could put forward excuses, but in teaching, it was not possible. So for the days I did not have tuition teaching, I used to go to the library. I had a membership in Kollam Public Library also. These two centres, with the additional materials I had collected from

EFLU, provided ample sources of reference books for my studies and teaching.

Some girls in my tuition class were ardent fans of me. The advantage of young age and showing knowledge in literature and, moreover, the cracks of jokes made them my dear ones. If need be, I could make them my soulmates. But I never wanted to treat them more than my dear students.

I remembered one of my previous experiences as a guest teacher in a senior secondary school at Kannanalloor at Kottiyam. I was there for a month contract basis teaching due to the regular teacher being in childcare leave. I had to teach the eleventh and twelfth classes. A week after I started teaching there, on a Saturday, my class was on the third storey of the academic building for the Plus Two science class. At two forty-five, after two periods of post-lunch sessions, the bell rang for the day, and the pupils got ready to go home. Downstairs, on the corridor on the left, a cute girl was waiting with her friend and called me to stop. The angel-like girl came to me and asked to my astonishment, 'Will you marry me?' I just smiled it away and took it as a childish whim. I never told this to anybody in the school. I feared that if I did so, the girl would become a laughingstock for the entire school. So I never disclosed this to anybody. How couldn't I have been like that as I wore the coat of a teacher from the age of 18?

But here, a classmate of mine shattered my heart completely.

The next day, she told me the cause of her absence on the previous day. She had fever. I asked her wittily, 'Were you afraid of the letter?'

She nodded. She told me that the letter really crushed her feelings of being innocent and caused cold and fever, so she had gone to a hospital; that was why she was absent yesterday.

'But tell me, are you indeed a comrade?' she asked me.

'Why?' I queried.

'Because comrades love truth and do anything for their ends. Whatever they say, they would like to do it. They don't have any faith in god. They don't have any religion. They believe in truth only. They believe only in humanity. Are you a communist, Nilesh?'

'My heart is a communist's heart. But I don't want to follow it blindly. An ideology two centuries old needs some reforms like all the age-old religions of the world.'

'Sorry daa . . .' It was a sorry that should have come from me but came from her instead. It was an indication of her affection towards me.

'Where is the reply?' I asked her a little later.

'I really fell ill after writing the reply. I don't know why. Here is my reply.' She gave me her 'fake' letter.

Accepting it, I asked her, 'Is it a fake one?'

'Thu pahale isko pakado fir nirnaylelo.' She insisted to read it first and then take the decision.

With the letter in my pocket, I sneaked out of the class that had not yet started and went up to the rooftop of the academic block, where usually nobody came, so that no one would disturb me.

I opened the letter and began to read it.

My breath and my eyeball Nilesh, I want to say this: I really like you, and I really love you. I really worship you.

You are the idol in the temple of my heart. I offer you my sacred heart as the four walls to protect the idol. No rain, no storm, no famine, no religious riots can uproot you from there. I give you offerings and light the chandelier in front of you every moment of my life. You shower your affection and love on me always. I am the greedy one before you, offering a bouquet of love roses to you. What a lovely thing you are! My life's fulfilment, it seems to me, rests in you. All other relations are really necessary for our existence. But this love is an extra. Its feelings and passions are making our life meaningful. It is not a condition of life but a decoration of it, and I decide to adorn my life with it. It is only goodness an adornment can give me, and so I say again that we can hope more from the love relation.

I am made from you, and so I belong to you and you only. We can start a new relation, a deep relation, and an unbroken bond of love that our lives can make.

I for you and you for me; in between us, the petals of love create a bed of roses that spreads the fragrance all around us.

I can't name the thing that made me love you. I simply say this: I can't live without you.

The letter sucked the virginity of her heart, and first she fell in sick and later in lovesickness.

After reading the letter, I could not believe it myself. I touched my cheek to sense it and recognize myself that I was not in a daydream. All of a sudden, I realized that I got only a fake love letter. What was written, it was just for the sake of our agreement and not meant for genuineness. That recognition depressed me a lot. I thought about what reply I would give her if she would ask my opinion about the fake letter. Later on, I thought about her previous words that she had a fever after writing her reply.

If it was a fake letter, why did she have a fever? I thought.

Just before I entered the class, I overheard Nimmy talking with Shilpa about me. She admitted to Shilpa that she really loved me.

'What can I do, Shilpa? I am feeling so restless. He has plucked my heart. I can't simply avoid him. The letter I gave him was not a fake one. It was my real feelings for him. What's your opinion on it?'

'The door of the heart opens from inside and can't be locked from outside. What is happening is not controlled by us,' Shilpa replied in a confirmative way.

'Sometimes I too feel the same, I can't simply avoid him. When he came to my mind is unknown to me. His selfless simplicity, virtuous innocence, and considerate feelings attracted me. By the by, don't tell him about it.'

I heard it. I did not go back to the class. I left the classroom. I couldn't control my happiness. I felt I was on top of the world. For the last two semesters, I had been running after her. Now what I had desired had happened. I had to follow her till she began to chase me. Now her chase after me has begun. For the last two hours, I didn't turn up for the class.

She rang me. 'Where are you, Nilesh?'

'Here in the college canteen. What happened?'

'Madam is enquiring after you.'

'Which madam?'

I sensed the temperature of love fever had begun to stir in her heart. I felt love is like demise; once it happens, it buries all our hardships and begins a new opening.

From then on until after ten thirty in the night, we conversed through our mobiles. We were planning a good and prosperous life. Sometimes combined study by sharing study materials via CS application. Life in imagination is so sweet and tempts others to dream. We shared our feelings and companionship through our e-gadgets. Instant photos of ours were exchanged through WhatsApp. I gave her a complete photographic detail of my life at home. She too shared hers. During the end of the third semester of our course, our attachment grew beyond the clouds. We began to share our meals, studies, and love at the same quantity.

One March night, I was calling her in a very secretive and happy mood. I came out of my house. There was a full moon. I felt the moon rained over me its silver light; it chilled my heart. She told me I was pouring over her sweet and fragrant words that made her lovesick. Nature was so lustrous in the night. I told her to open the window and look out at the rain of moonlight. Even the trees and grass were transformed by the silvery beam, then how humans could not be taken part in it, especially the lovesick birds. That day, nature created its fabulous bed for us and then took away with it our sleep.

CHAPTER 10

During the last and final semester of the course, our relation reached the summit of seventh heaven and excitement. We really began to exist for each other. We realized that one could not live without the other.

Just three months left before our final exam would begin. Nimmy invited all of us to her house to celebrate a festival.

It opened an opportunity to go to her house and meet her family once again. My first visit to my sweetheart's house was on the occasion of her ancestral temple's festival. I took the initiative of booking an eight-seater Scorpio a day before the trip. I prepared the list of goers and organized the journey.

According to the plan, we assembled at the college junction at ten in the morning. As it was Sunday, there was no hustle and bustle of the office-goers and students. In the morning, I had class in the Cooperative College. Actually, the class time was from 10 a.m. to 1 p.m., but I had requested Madam Laisa, the principal in charge of the tutorial, to shift the time for my convenience, so the class was arranged from 7.30 to 9.30 a.m.

Just after the class, I dialled my friends to confirm their arrival on time. First, I contacted Reshmi.

She laughed at me, commenting, 'How are you interested in her case?'

'Tell me where you are.'

'On the way . . . Within ten minutes, I will be there. Daaaa.'

'What about the others?'

'I contacted Shalini. She is not coming as she has to shoot an episode today.'

'She informed me the same yesterday. Okay . . . Let's meet at the college junction.'

At around nine forty-five, I had reached the college junction. The first thing I did was call the driver of our car. He assured me that he would reach there at ten thirty as scheduled earlier.

I parked my bike at the side of a kiosk under the great banyan tree and went to the College House, a restaurant in the SN College junction, which I saw was functioning even on Sunday. The restaurant was a haunting place for me. It was one of the rare restaurants in the area where the staff and food remained the same for years. I had heard one of my professors, Mr Salim Kumar, remarked that when he was a student at the college, he often used to dine at the restaurant. Even today, the restaurant had not changed much, especially in the matter of the colour and taste of the food and even the waiters there. The only change that sometimes happened there was the change of the man in the cashier seat. I was also a regular visitor there for my lunch, so I had the freedom to sit there at any length.

We had decided to assemble there for our journey. As it was a holiday, the regular rush was not there in the restaurant. I entered the waiting lounge of the café and waited for the others to turn up, spending time at the dailies spread over there. Till Robin's arrival, my companions remained the newspapers on the lounge sofa. As we sat down there, the next member came.

'Hi . . . Nilesh, when did you get here?' Reshmi arrived.

'Ten minutes before . . .' I looked at her. 'Wow! You are looking wonderful in that dress.' I appreciated her dress.

'Thank you for your admiration. What about the others?'

'All are on their way. Within few minutes, they will be here.'

'Tell me, Nilesh, what are you going to give her today?' she asked.

'What?' I replied with another query.

'Why, it is your maiden visit there, so you are supposed to give some gift to her.'

'Tell me what gift I should give her rather than going myself to her house.'

As our chat progressed, the number of group members was also increasing; Shilpa and Seemol came together.

The last one to join our group was Fatima. I had contacted Apsy a little earlier, and he told me he was waiting at the high school junction. So the entire group was ready for the trip. I rang the car driver. In the meantime, we came out of the restaurant to the pedestrian way of NH 47. It was just a half an hour drive from the college junction to Nimmy's house at Chavara. The car came within a few minutes of the phone call to where we were waiting. Robin and I sat in the front seat.

Reshmi asked Robin, 'Why don't you come here and sit with us?'

'How can he? He is afraid of her.' The explanation came from Seemol.

'*Podi* . . . She is afraid of me,' Robin retorted.

The band of ladies in fine festive clothes sat in the middle row.

The journey started. After two minutes of driving, we had to halt just opposite of the clock tower at Chinnakada for traffic clearance. The clock tower was just like a pointing finger raised towards the sky, showed the time to be eleven o'clock. For the people of Kollam, this clock tower is like a reminder of their past glory. In Kerala history, time began with Kollam, and the clock tower was a monument for the past glory.

As the journey resumed after getting the traffic signal, I received a call from Nimmy.

From the caller's end, she asked, 'Where are you? Didn't start the journey yet?'

I answered, 'We are on the way, and within half an hour, we will reach there. Did the functions start there?'

'It's going to begin.' As she answered, my phone showed a waiting call from Apsy.

Nimmy confirmed our arrival and said bye.

I called Apsy back and told him to come in front of Annapurna Hotel where we were approaching.

We picked him up from there and gave him the rear seat beside with Fatima.

On the way, we commented on our dress and listened to the low-voiced music from the FM radio.

At eleven o'clock, it was the time for 98.3 FM Radio Mirchi's Hindi melodies. The evergreen song 'Sagar Jaisi Aankhon Wali' filled the chilled air of the car chalet. The beginning of the song obviously brought a silence to our talk. It reminded me of the sweet breeze that blows in the evenings of December along the Kollam sea beach that flows through thousands gathered there to chat and hear the wave's song in a low pitch. The breeze brings to even the isolated minds a magic spell to dream and be romantic in life.

Before the song came to an end, we reached the courtyard of Nimmy's ancestral home. People were busy with several activities. We saw three elephants in front of the courtyard. They had been bathed and were being fed by their mahouts. A little crowd of children in front of them was watching in wonder the big round of rice being brought to the elephants' mouths. Elephant feeding was a wonderful sight for the children. Some were on the veranda and on the courtyard, enjoying the rare sight.

A man in his early fifties came to us and welcomed us. '*Varin makkale* [welcome, children] . . . Nimmy told us about you. I am her uncle, the eldest one in the family.'

At one part of the house, a pandal was erected for supplying the meal. Nimmy's house was a newly built two-storey building with all the modern amenities in it.

My eyes were probing for her, and immediately I got a mind reading message to look up the quadrangular balcony there. She was in a traditional Kasavu sari, with a sandal paste mark on her forehead, and was smiling heartily to welcome us. She smiled from among the flowers there in the balcony garden. She looked like a rose among the flower garden. Both she and the flowers smiled alike, and it was difficult for me to distinguish between them. I felt that her smile sprouted from her heart, eyes, and lips together. The smile was a combination of a rare fragrance that spread in the surrounding ambience which was more festive than the real festival. I gazed at her with the wonder of a vineyard tourist seeing the grape-bearing vines for the first time. I felt her smile fell on me and me alone like a soft shower of chill in the summer heat. I caught the smile and casketed it in the last chest of my heart as a treasure for my whole life.

She came down to the veranda and took us to the drawing room. She welcomed her friends with a hearty, audible laugh and introduced her father, Mr Nanda Kishore, and mother, Professor Sreedevi. Her father was the manager of SBI's Sasthamcottah branch, and her mother was a professor of English literature in the Devaswom Board College of Sasthamcottah.

Later, Nimmy introduced us to her family. After the preface ritual, the female group was taken to the interior of the house to see her bedroom and personal collections in it.

Nimmy's mother brought drinks for us, and as we were taking it, her father excused himself to go out for his work as somebody wanted to meet him.

I looked around to see the beautifications in the hall; some family pictures hung on the wall like the little drops of frozen memories. The computer table was placed in one corner just opposite of the wall TV, and the monitor was still winking the Google web portal for its user.

Her younger sister came there and talked with us. She recognized me among the group.

'How do you know me?' I asked.

'We met at the railway station when we came to pick up Nimmy Chechi,' she replied.

'So you never forgot us?'

'No. I used to watch your Facebook posting.'

'But you are not a friend of mine in Facebook.'

'No, no, I saw it in Nimmy Chechi's account. Your postings are really good.' She appreciated me.

She had good confidence for eye contact with us and talked with us freely, a quality I liked most in Nimmy too.

A lot of guys, like me, actually prefer girls that wear less make-up. We like the natural beauty in girls. Both these sisters were simple and modest, with a lot of people skills that made them dear to the whole village, which I could read from the gathering of locals there.

'Please come, lunch is ready,' Nimmy called us.

'At this time?' Robin wondered after looking at the clock there, which told it was only 11.30 a.m.

'The procession has to start at one o'clock in the afternoon. After that, there will be no meals till the procession ends at the temple,' she reasoned.

Meanwhile, I rang the driver to invite him for the meal. He told me that somebody had forced him to sit at the pandal for meals. I replied that was good.

We were led to the dining hall where a feast of *sadya* was ready. The traditional Keralite sadya, a vegetarian meal of boiled rice, crispy *papad*, serving curries, and a host of side dishes and desserts, was served on a plantain leaf as custom demanded. Nimmy sat just opposite to me and was serving us like a mature housewife and simultaneously having her meal with us.

There was no lack for talk and laughter during the time. It was really an enjoyable day in our life. Nimmy and her family treated us as real guests. I so felt their hospitality. I remembered the Indian philosophy 'Atithi devo bhava'. We really felt it here.

Towards the end of the sadya, the *ada payasam*, the hot dessert of Kerala was served by Nimmy's mother. After that, a few of us tasted buttermilk, and some of us tasted rasam, a soup using tamarind juice as a base. Nimmy and I tasted both as the end dish. The natural taste of the rasam gave me a chance to wink at her without the others noticing. She liked it and expressed it through her eyes, widely opening them like a supersonic jet.

The food we had from there had the taste of love in it, so it turned into a special treat for me.

The meal was over by quarter past twelve in the afternoon. Nimmy's uncle announced for the stoppage of serving the Ashtami Rohini feast till the procession had reached the sanctum sanctorum of the Krishna Temple. Along with the famous festival of Ashtami Rohini in Guruvayur Temple, a miniature form of the festival was going to be conducted there in their ancestral temple of Lord Krishna.

The auspicious moments of Vilakku Ezhunnelippu to the temple was then going to begin. Nimmy, in Kasavu sari, came and took the handheld, lighted oil lamp from the pedestal of tulsi plant, the family shrine, and lighted the first wick of the seven layers of the *deepasthambam* lamp that was set in the eastern side of the courtyard. As she lighted up the first wick of the chandelier, the drum-beaters began their Sinkari Melam that lasted till the playing of Pancha Vadya Melam. One by one, she and her sister lighted all the wicks of the seven-tier lamp. That was the formal beginning of the Vilakku Ezhunnelippu. The lamp was lifted and took a pious round in the Tulsi podium to mark the beginning of the procession. As the lamp was lifted, the womenfolk made an auspicious howling. Nimmy's uncle led the procession to the temple. Four able-bodied men took the deepasthambam to a wooden podium and preceded the entire pilgrims to the sanctum sanctorum of Panachavila Sree Krishna Swami Temple, the ancestral temple of the Panachavila family, with the accompaniment of three caparisoned tuskers and a large crowd of devotees. As the procession moved forward, the number of following devotees began to increase.

The procession began to move towards the temple. The deepasthambam bearers were at the front portion of the procession. It was followed by all the family members, friends, temple festival committee members, and other devotees accompanying the lamp. Behind it, the Panchavadyam players made up the third row of the procession, and the drum-beaters followed suit. At the last of the procession were the three caparisoned tuskers in a line.

Everyone left the house except Nimmy and us, the guests, and a few outside workers of her house. Nimmy came inside and told us to take a rest for a while.

She winked at me to go along with her. I accompanied her upstairs, and she led me to her bedroom. She welcomed me to her bedroom and asked me, 'How do you feel here?'

'A divine beauty in everything that you do, how nice to live in such a family,' I replied.

'Are you not a communist?'

'What is in it? Can't a communist love a pious girl?'

'I don't know how much I love you, Nilesh. Really, I'm madly in love with you.' Saying this, she embraced me just like a schoolgoing girl hugs her mother. There was not even a thin layer of air in between our bodies; she believed in me that much. I put my arms around her to convey all the love I could to her.

'You are my breath, you are my life. Without you, I am only a pool of tears,' I murmured to her ears.

This was the real moment of love fulfilment. How difficult it was to get a girl of her nature in love. A girl of such a firm familial context never could be slipped into an easy love relation. I knew she was expecting from me an affection equal to that which the entire family members together could give her. She saw in me her own family's love. I was so cool. I was so satisfied. I was so content. I felt I was the one so loved in the entire humanity. She hugged me as lovingly as a flower holds its fragrance into its petals. I felt around me the fragrance of a maiden flower. It made the room a place so near to heaven. We shared the music of our hearts. She whispered in my ears, 'How much do you love me?'

'I'm not just loving you, I am caring for you like a mother cares for her baby in the womb. I love you like a river loves its own water, I love you like a sea loves the beach with an unbroken and continuous patting with love, and I love you like the sun loves the sea and part every day with red eyes to see her in the morning and make her glitter.'

Love is not a moment of passion but a moment of understanding.

Somebody from the back courtyard was calling, 'Nimmymoleeee? Nimmymoleeee?'

She looked at my heart through my eyes and smiled through her eyes. Then she answered the call, 'Sumathiamma, keep it in the store, we are moving to temple now.'

She moved her body from mine after transferring her warmth and scent on me.

'Let's go for the temple,' she asked me.

'Hh.' I nodded in half-mindly.

She repeated her query, 'Let's go for the temple.'

'Of course,' I added. She led me to down the stairs. Love made me giddy in my head.

We came to the hall where our friends were waiting for us.

'Let's follow the procession?' she requested of them.

Everyone looked at one another, and Robin asked, 'How much distance from here?'

'Just a chat walk from here,' she kidded. 'Come, let us walk.'

The sound of *asuravadya* (drum) was still lingering in the air. We moved to the road. The way to the temple was decorated with a large number of lit oil lamps on either side of the street to adorn the premises of the temple and welcome the festival procession. The lights, luminous in the banyan trees, and all the vendors of balloons and playthings for children make the street busy. Pedestrians and bike-riders and car-goers were driving along the street in a cautious way to avoid any unwanted incidents.

The children were seen pulling their parents towards the exhibition stands of the balloon vendors. The most attractive thing was the hydrogen balloons that stand up in the sky to liberate from its holder and reach its lover's bosom. All hydrogen balloons were lovers that wanted to be unfettered from all the restrictions of their life and float in the sky with their spouse, the white clouds in the sky. I thought the heart-shaped balloons wanted this. The children were their releasers.

By the time we reached the temple along with the procession, a large crowd of people was there to witness it. This lamp procession took place once in three years. We stood at a little distance and watched all the proceedings there. At this time, my mobile began to ring. I took it and looked at it; the driver was calling us to return. I didn't answer it because it was not audible in the general chaos of the Sinkari Melam. A long queue was set in front of the temple for a darshan of the deity.

Before we left the place, Nimmy looked at me and gave me a considerate smile. I saw in her eyes a sea of affection that made its ripples in them.

CHAPTER 11

Our final-semester exam was over on 19 April. Our elective paper, ELT, was the last exam. At one o'clock in the afternoon, the exam was over. We realized with an ache that we had to discontinue college from tomorrow onwards. From tomorrow onwards, we would become alumni of the college. We felt so sorry to leave the campus that gifted us this cheerful bond. After the exam was over, we assembled once again in the class like on the valedictory day function we celebrated one and a half months ago and shared our bond of friendship, pledging further meetings in the coming days of our lives.

Even Apsy suffered the pain of parting. We embraced each other and consoled ourselves.

The first one who left our group was Shalini. She had an episode to shoot in the Vellayambalam Asianet Plus studio. She excused herself from us for her withdrawal. She asked us to call her for the live-shoot show that was going to air soon.

I brought a special valedictorian gift for Nimmy on the day—a glassy icon of a deer rubbing its right eye on the sharp edge of a buck which tells the trust of a man–woman relationship. In return, she gave her fancy chain to me. I took it and held it in my right hand for a long time and later dropped it into my chest pocket. Even after everyone went away, we alone were left there, crying and consoling ourselves. When Ramettan came there to shut the doors at around three thirty in the afternoon, we had to leave the classroom.

I took her on the pillion of my bike and rode to Chinnakada to see her off. Before we bid adieu, we went to Ice World Cookies in Jerome Nagar for a chat over an ice cream. We ordered fruit desserts one after another and shared them, then went on sitting, tasting, looking, and sharing our passions. We discussed our future. The discussion ended on the common decision of a marriage proposal. We planned for our marriage.

At around five thirty in the evening, her cell rang. Her mother was on the caller's end. She gave the excuse that she had a function in the college and was now on the way. I dropped her at the bus stop and saw her off. I really felt the pain of a departing relation, even though we would have chances of contacting each other.

When the meetings together ended with the course, we adopted other ways by which we could continue our rendezvous. All the e-communication networks connected us the entire time. Her parents sensed our love from these e-communications. As they knew me earlier, they agreed to the proposal of marriage. They enquired Nimmy about me. She told them that I was all alone and that my only brother was in Qatar. Knowing this, they showed reluctance to the proposal, saying that it would be a crisis for her in the future. But with her pressure, they agreed to proceed with the proposal.

While waiting for the final results, I got a chance to teach in a PSC coaching institute at Kollam. I was getting a decent remuneration for the competitive exam classes than from tuition classes. The money and future utility of contesting in competition tests for a profession encouraged me to work hard for the classes. I too felt a permanent government job was necessary to get a girl like her.

Just two weeks left for the publication of our final results. One morning, Nimmy called me to inform me of her parents' decision to visit my home.

I felt a little apprehension due to the comparison of the two families. She had been blessed with all the relations in her life. Both her parents were gazette-ranked employees. Her house was a big one, suitable for the kind of people in the front row of the society. She followed a well-established system in her life. Even though her parents were not so orthodox, they should have their own likeness and cultural set-up. I could not count the scale of expectations they kept in their minds for their future son-in-law. I had only my good character and personality and hard work for achieving my goal. I had already started preparations for UGC-Net and, at the same time, for an employment in the government sector. Four months ago, I did the competitive test for parliament assistant and was now waiting for the results.

I thought about both our castes. Did her parents know about my caste? We shared one religion but had different castes. She belonged to the upper caste list of a Nair, and I belonged to the OBC list—an Ezhava. We had never asked about our castes before. Did her parents know about it? Would they permit us to unite? A lot of confusion arose in my mind. But I was sure that we share the same breath; share the same sights; share the same dreams; share the same country; share the same feelings, passion, and love; and live under the same jurisdiction.

I decided to welcome them into my uncle's house. Even though it was a small one, it was a decent-looking house for people like Nimmy's father. I informed the same to Kuttathy, the elder daughter of my uncle. She was so considerate in my affairs. She sometimes treated me like her own son even though she was not that much old. She agreed to convey the message to her father and got the permission for the bridal party's house-visiting observance.

After getting the consent from my uncle, I phoned Nimmy to convey the proceedings in my house. She informed me her father and her maternal uncle would visit my house on the coming Sunday.

I asked her, 'At what time?'

'That I will inform you later,' she replied.

She told me to ready myself to receive them. She let me know her parents were ready to accept her choice after her pressure on them.

On Saturday evening, I got her on chat.

'Hi . . . Nimmy dear, what's going on there?'

'Nothing, da.'

'Tell me, at what time r they coming here?'

'Afternoon.'

'Do they know the route?'

'Up to Parippally, no problem.'

'I will pick them up from there. I arranged it in my uncle's house, da.'

'No problem.'

'Before they set out, you just call me.'

'Sure, da . . .'

'Where is your cell?'

'On my side.'

'Okay, I'll call you now.'

'All right.'

I took my cell and rang her to get more information on their visit details. We talked for half an hour about her parents' friendly approach with them. And both she and Kavu pressured their father for the proposal.

'I really want to say that people like your father are very rare. Otherwise, on what background would he have agreed to marry his daughter to me? In marriage relations, family has a big part to play, especially the father and mother. I don't have both, yet that your parents are ready to accept your choice is a bit of good fortune for me. I will always be an obedient son to them instead of a son-in-law.' I got a little bit emotional in the subject. I told her, 'My mother was also like your father, a candid human.'

That day we had no time to talk about our UGC-Net preparation. Usually, we chatted on previous question papers from UGC-Net. She always promoted me to pass net or secure a job that she believed would make our relation easier. We ended our talk with a sweet and hot virtual kissing.

On Sunday morning, I woke up a little earlier and got ready for a two-hour class in Excellent Tutorial at Parippally. Sir Baiju had asked me for an examination round-up class for the Plus Two students of Amrita Vidyalaya whose English exam was extended due to a general strike called by the LDF. Within two hours, the entire question patterns, possible questions, and a revision of the syllabus had to be taught by me. It was a pre-planned session, so I went there to teach the class. Moreover, it was a place where I met my local friends. I arrived there at eight thirty, half an hour before the scheduled time of the class. My intention was just to make a friendly talk with my friends Monish and Pakru. KV was the director in charge of the tutorial. I had told Sir Baiju and Sir Monish about the proposed visit of Nimmy's father in the evening. I requested them to be in my uncle's house in the evening as my kith and kin. They with pleasure agreed to come. I needed someone to talk with Nimmy's father and her uncle. I felt I needed help to talk with them formally other than my uncle. So I invited them. They had already married and had the experience of handling such situations. Moreover, both of them were government employees. Sir Baiju was working as a Plus Two teacher in an aided school, and Sir Monish was working as a Secretariat assistant. I thought they would be good company for the visiting guests. At eleven thirty, the class was over, and before I left there, I reminded both of my special guests of the invitation.

Usually, the proposal went from the boy's house to the girl's. But here, as the groom had already visited the bride's house, it was the choice of the bride's party to visit the groom's house. Moreover, Nimmy's father had to take a final decision in this matter after visiting my home. In all matters, her family was far up than mine.

That day I had my lunch in my uncle's house. Auntie Savithri told me yesterday itself to come for lunch. They were very accommodating people, just like the staff of the cooperative tutorials, where I got enough motherly concern from a handful of madams like Laisa, Sunanda, Remani, and Ganga, the teaching faculty there. The secretary of the institute, Madam Annamma, was a real creative critic of me. She was a frankly speaking woman.

At around three o'clock in the afternoon, Nimmy called me.

'Hi, Nimmy, did they set out?' I enthusiastically asked.

'Yes, just now. My dad and uncle. You may go to Parippally to pick them up. I have given them your number.'

'Oh sure . . . In which car are they coming?'

'White Hyundai Verna.'

'Okay.'

'How much time would it take to reach there?'

'Maximum of one hour, if there is no traffic block. By the by, is there any objection from your parents?'

'My choice is first as it is my life.'

'That's okay, but any unlike?'

'Naturally, it affects their ego. Never mind it. Tell your uncle to be so polite and considerate.'

'That's okay daaa.'

'Nilesh, I want to ask you a simple question.'

'What is it? Ask me.'

'Now tell me how much you love me.'

This was the second time she asked me the same question.

'I have a plan in my mind that we don't go to sleep for more than six hours a day. We have to utilize the maximum time in our life by waking up like early birds and looking together, laughing together, watching together, going on outings together, cooking together, eating together, and making love together because I love you that much. I flutter around you always in my life like a butterfly soars around a blossoming garden. You are promising me an all-season garden of variety and sweet aroma in my life forever and ever. Life for us means celebration of each and every moment in our togetherness. Even in sleep, I want to see dreams about you. I gave my life to you as I know you are the only custodian of it. In the same way, I have taken yours. You have given me your life for my own care and protection. My love to you can't be expressed in words. If so, they need blood and sensation. If words have existence, they can reveal my love to you.' After a pause, I asked her, 'Are you listening to me?'

'Yesssssss . . . Now, dear, go to the appointed place and receive them.'

'Okay da.'

I told my uncle I was going to receive them. I took my bike and went to Parippally Junction to en route them to my uncle's home. A large number of beautiful and company-sent cars were flying up and down the NH 47. I waited for the one in which the decision of my future life rested. I had already informed Nimmy that I would be waiting in front of the Rajakumari Wedding Centre on the Paravoor roadside. They had to take the right turn at the peepul tree traffic circle.

Within a few minutes, a Verna took the right turn and Nimmy's papa came into my view. I waved at them to stop and convoyed them to my uncle's house. Within a few minutes' drive, we reached our destination. The car was parked inside the courtyard of the house. As they came out from the car, my uncle welcomed them to the house. Sir Baiju and Sir Monish had already come there.

The first thing that the guests' eyes got stuck on was the portrait of Sree Narayana Guru in the podium of worship placed in the hall. They observed it with certain uncertainties in their minds. Nimmy's papa asked me, 'Mr Nilesh, in which caste do you belong to?' I simply told him my caste. All of a sudden, I noticed the rapid flush in his face. As he belonged to a Nair family, he could not accept the proposal. He expressed his dislike straightforwardly.

He said regretfully, 'Even after all the hardships you had in your life, I thought, Nilesh, you belong to my own caste.'

These words were a genuine shock for both parties.

I had never told Nimmy my caste or she had never asked me. We never thought it would become an unbreakable fence between us.

Hastily, even without having tea and snacks, they came out of the house.

Within a second, the castle of cards collapsed with a bang in my heart. For a few minutes, I couldn't understand what was going on there. Nimmy's father said sorry to my uncle for disturbing him and turned towards the car and left there.

My friends were too shocked to ask me the reason. No civilized human could act like this in the name of anything. I felt humiliated by his actions. I could not understand his mentality. Even at this age of advancement, meeting people that think in terms of caste and religion, especially the educated ones, was really a shocking experience for me.

At least he can accept the hospitality that we provide them, I thought to myself.

I couldn't understand the frank mentality of the so-called people talking about religion and caste. When it comes to one's own issues, man is selfish; otherwise, he will talk about noble causes.

If he has doubt about my caste, he could have enquired earlier and taken a decision. Why this at the eleventh hour of all development? my logic asked.

What would happen if he proposed a boy from another caste? One's caste or religion does not make one lesser in status to another according to the new pattern of society. The leaders of these two communities are constantly demanding for a wider Hindu blending. Humanity is still in the primitive age. The primitive triggers were still in our blood, or we were consciously generating them in us. The scientific discoveries brought any changes in human mentality other than physical appearance and material wealth. *The primitiveness still wheels us*, I thought.

I reflected on our love. It had no primitiveness. It had a rhythm and music. It was a source of solace for me in the lonely path of my life. For us, romance was not at all a false dream. It did not have the taste or colour of caste. It took its birth in our minds when one heart began to know the other. Ours was not a physical infatuation of passion but an understanding of each other.

The sea can love only the sky. The sea never loves another sky. They exchange their love in a natural language. She sends her love in the form of vapour. And he sends it back in rains. That's why when the rain falls on the sea, it sings a melody. Their romance has music and solace in it. They will share love with each other for ages yet to be counted. It will remain the same for all ages to come. This is the solemn face of love in nature. We as well were like them in an exalted romance, but within seconds, everything went topsy-turvy. Dark clouds began to bar our union.

Except humans, no other animal on earth knows the high drama of acting. He is the only creature on earth that uses a synthetic language. At any moment, he puts the dress of an actor and becomes a fake-language user. No men are exempt from this faculty except the true lovers. We were true lovers. We were like the sea and sky. Till the last drop of water in her basin, she was ready to send her romantic clouds to me, and I in return romantic rain. In between us, we didn't know any artificial language; ours was the true language of love and understanding. Even the grass and sand who had witnessed our love blushed and thrilled in our union. Even they had supported our romance. Such chaste love was ruined by the concept of caste.

'Ethrayo janmamai ninne jnan thedunnu. [For how many ages I have been searching for you] . . .' The special ringtone for Nimmy was playing on my cell.

'What happened da?' As I attended the phone, Nimmy asked me.

'Called your father?'

'Yes.'

'Just before taking the tea, he asked me about my caste, and I told him about it,' I began to explain.

'Then what happened?'

'Dear . . . Uncle became a strange man. He apologized to my uncle for the proposal and left the scene immediately. I think he doesn't like to marry his daughter away to another caste other than his own.' After a pause, I continued, 'Don't worry, dear, we can make him appreciate our affair one day.'

'Try our best.' Her voice was shaky.

'What did your dad tell you?'

She began to sob. I became silent.

'Dear . . .' I addressed her in the same passion.

'My father told me to forget you forever.' Her sobbing turned into crying, and she cancelled the call.

Everyone turned stiff and cold in the house like the Himalayan frost. My friends soothed me with patting and a few consoling phrases. I couldn't control the inner sob in my heart, and I began to walk towards my house. Kuttathy was calling me at my back. I heard her but couldn't stop. She came behind me and took me to her own house, which was adjacent to her ancestral home.

She consoled me, telling me, 'I know, Nilesh, your love for her. If she is predestined for you, nothing can object to it. Be happy, and think about your future.'

I heard nothing of her discourse because my mind was numb. I felt it like a virus attack on my brain. Her antivirus treatments couldn't replace the damaged cells of my brain. I felt Nimmy's father had whipped our love and threw us in a state of undying dejection.

'You are not yet at a marriageable age. I am sure she will wait for you. You know, in Hindu religion, there is no option to change your caste. Otherwise, we can think in terms of that. Dear son'—she sometimes called me like that even though she was not that much older than me—'Hindu is not a religion, but only a belief. I don't know why people believe so hard in beliefs. Sometimes abstract ideas overcome the concrete facts. I know your love is a concrete fact, but it is thwarted by false belief.' She turned philosophic to soothe my pain.

Our horoscope was matching, but three things were mismatching for us—caste, parents, and money.

Life is lived by two groups. One group live their lives with extras, and the other live with the minimum. All of us need air, water, sunlight, and food. They are not extras. A house is a necessity, but a large house is an extra. Dreams are perhaps a necessity because they made our DNA. But love is an extra. The love towards an extraordinary girl is distinctly an extra.

Was Nimmy an extra for me? Was our relation an extra for us? If it was extra, what was life then?

CHAPTER 12

I was enormously tired after the whole turnover in my life. I thought the mind of Nimmy's dad was built on certain biased feelings and not on love and humanity. It seemed religious belief to him was more than the cost of his own daughter.

The Hindu religion does not claim any one prophet or any one god, it does not believe in any one philosophic concept, and it does not follow any one act of religious rite or performance; in fact, it does not satisfy the traditional features of a religion or creed. It is a way of life, and nothing more. Yet people began to think in terms of the age-old traditional works that decided the castes in Hinduism and followed it. The real Hindus are atheists; they consider Hinduism as a philosophy. It puts forward a complex philosophy of samsara, karma, and moksha. It provides the follower freedom of belief and worship. Hinduism conceives the whole world as a single family. It believes in one truth. It accepts all forms of beliefs. Yet people like him kept this philosophy for their false pride. I felt sorry for it.

All religions preach about love, but when it comes to one's own affairs, one will forget the good sayings and preaching. Then he begins to think false prejudices and values. In reality, life is built on certain principles in which most humans weigh the status and fashion of people and not the loving and caring minds. Human qualities have less value in choosing a marital relationship. We become the tools of false prejudices of our own society. Where is equality of human life in Hinduism? It is only in the preaching, not in doing. Every human is selfish. That is why when they think in terms of their own children, they weigh all the false values of life. The status symbol begins to reign over their thoughts. Every human by nature is selfish. No religion supports prejudices, but humans conveniently interpret them as according to their need.

I tried to put aside the frustration with the optimistic concept that everything would be filtered out in the course of time because life for me has yet to start. I closed my eyes and prayed for my mother. She came to me in my dream and consoled me by patting my head; she put my head on her lap and, without saying anything, kissed my forehead. The only solace in my life was my dream and my mother. She comforted me like the mother hen keeping her chicks under her wings to protect them from the eagles' long-eye attack.

After half an hour's nap, I woke up. The comforting pat vanished from my mind. Once again, I came to a line of thought. It began to disturb me. My head turned into a nursery of thoughts. Once again, I thought of the world's earliest religion, Hinduism. If one Hindu cannot embrace another, how can they adopt reform? People say Hinduism is not a religion, but a way of life; if so, why do they grasp hold of the age-old system of tiers? It is not a religion of four tiers. But it is a religion of freedom. Hinduism doesn't implement any rules on its followers. It is itself subjected to change according to the passage of time. No other religion gives its followers this much freedom. Yet people were eager to follow certain discarded old-generation traditions. Hinduism gives its followers the freedom to choose the present set-up of the society by forgetting the false customs of the past. Reform is the base stone of Hinduism. If there is no possibility for reform, Hinduism will remain the worst faith in the world.

The Hindu religion needs reform in its basic set-up. The system of hierarchy should be banished from it. The followers celebrate the same festival, go to the same temples, worship the same deities, live in the same land, follow the same culture, breathe the same air, have the same blood run in their veins, follow the same family culture, live under the same constitution, share the same dreams, and drink the same water, yet there are different tiers that have created the separation of the people. Promotion of inter-caste marriage is the only solution for it. For that purpose, we have to redefine our own mindset.

A Hindu and a Kerala communist are alike. Both believe in god. A communist's belief in god is only for his mind's peace. It is a source of comfort for him from his personal worries. A communist believes that the concept of god arises in a Hindu from the fear of death and destitution. If he can avoid the fear of destitution and death, he will also become a communist.

It's the land of the great Mahatma, who fought for the entire population and not for any sectarian society. The new-generation leaders even praise the sectarian progress as social work. If you consider only your own caste or religion or a sectarian community, how can you call it humanitarian work?

I remembered the fiery discussion Nimmy and Kavu had with their father. They agreed with him that he had given them all the freedom in their life. No restriction was there for them to do what they wanted to do.

Nimmy yesterday asked her father, 'What is wrong with Nilesh? Is it his caste? Is it his family? Is it his job? Or is it his house and money? Whatever it is, I am never going to mind it. I like only his personal qualities. If you can't agree with me, I will go and join in any of the hermit nuns of the Christian church.'

It is true that when love enters through the window, the wisdom leaps out through the door. Had she lost her wisdom? Whether she was talking with her parents in the right way, I doubted it, but I couldn't realize it because I was also in such a mood that I couldn't recognize what the parents wanted their children to do.

Somewhere in the middle of the big house of our hearts, a white dove was flapping. The hope was shattering somewhere in the rush of feelings of others who wanted to protect certain false values in life in the name of caste.

I learnt that Nimmy's father was an active member of his community and a possible candidate to the coming election of the NSS core committee at Chengannur. It might be the reason for his rejection of the proposal. But whatever it should be, it could not simply be acceptable.

The next day witnessed a shower of rain in the early morning. I just woke up and sat down in my cot, listening to the rain. I decided to see and listen to the rain, so I opened a side of the window. The rain reminded me of the English and Foreign Languages University professor Miss Julu Zen's habit of writing letters to her mother in Kolkata during rainy days. I too began to think of the rain. The soft falling rain created a soft tempo on the leaves of colocasia plants, which I was looking at through the window. The raindrops were falling and splitting themselves in an act of suicide. The soft falling showers have something to tell me I guess, but I could not begin to understand it. When the mind is disturbed with some worries, it is difficult to understand the language of nature.

I was totally lethargic that day. I pulled my bed sheet around me to warm up from the chilly weather outside. For the last five years I had been living alone in the house. My only companion was my red bed sheet, which I had bought with my first salary around five years ago. It was so attached with my feelings. I sometimes used to call it my partner. It wiped away my loneliness and, on occasions, 'talked' with me with its soft touches. It was a sweet memory for me and a real companion in sleep. In chilly days, if I didn't cuddle with it with my whole body, it would grumble at me. Sometimes it allowed the frosty breeze to disturb my feet and then began to giggle. We were really good friends. Even in the washing session, I gave it special care. It was 'bathed' alone when all other clothes of mine were washed together.

My Chettayi yesterday phoned me to enquire about the proposal. He was also sad of the happenings. He talked about the necessity of a new house for us. I too agreed with him. Now he was paid handsomely by his company and was capable of responsible thinking. Salary made him a mature and responsible elder. He had asked me whether I needed any money.

A cord of thoughts occurred in my mind. The hangover of the condemnation of our love affair was still lingering in my mind. I was about to go to the kitchen to prepare my tea when my cell phone rang; I had kept it in the window side. I looked at it in the sense of who was calling me this early morning. It showed: 'Shilpa calling . . .' So I attended the call.

'Hello, Nilesh.' In a very serious tone, she began to tell me, 'I got bad news now.' She stopped for a pause.

A ball of fire rolled through my heart. I asked her, 'Tell me, what is it?'

'Don't get upset.' She tried to prepare me for her news.

'Shilpa, please tell me. Don't make me panic,' I expressed my eagerness. At the same time, a rush of ill thoughts appeared in my mind.

'According to the latest information, there is nothing to be worried at present.' She went about it in a roundabout way that really put me in more confusion.

'What happened?' I begged her.

'Yesterday night, Nimmy's father tried to suicide.' Her voice was broken.

'*What*?' My voice got stuck.

'Yes. He has been hospitalized,' she clarified the incident.

'Why did he do it? For what?' I asked her in shock.

'I don't know the reason. Perhaps some argument went on regarding your relation,' she guessed.

The other end of love is not death but sacrifice, the sacrifice of love itself. When I heard the news of her father's suicide attempt, a tremor occurred in my heart. I thought about Nimmy, her pure heart. How could she bear it? In the name of love, she might become the reason for the death of her own father, whom she loved most and considered as the dearest in her household relations. Whenever she talked about him, she had a double heart. She loved and considered him as her role model in life. Whenever she talked about the good qualities in me, she used to make a metaphor of them with his. Theirs was an unconditional relation. She could not simply disregard it.

I remembered the good familial tie-up that Nimmy's household had. As a father, he gave full freedom to his children. There were no restrictions on his daughters in their personal choices. He was always a good friend to them. His attempted suicide was beyond expectation and imagination.

A lot of thoughts occurred in my heart. 'Where is he now?' I asked Shilpa.

'First, he was taken to Lilavati Hospital at Sasthamcottah, then he was referred to Trivandrum Medical College, but they took him to the KIMS hospital in Trivandrum,' she explained the seriousness of the case.

'Did you contact anyone from her house?' I eagerly quizzed.

'One of her close relatives gave me the information. According to the hospital authorities, nothing could be predicted about him, he is in such a critical condition.'

'Did you know anything about Nimmy?'

'She was in the hospital herself.'

'Shilpa, can you contact her? And if possible, do it for me. I terribly want to meet her immediately.'

'But, Nilesh, we can't expect how their relatives will react when they see you there. So please wait till tomorrow.'

'I don't think it is possible. You know how we were after his visit to my house. She would never attend my call till she would get permission from her father. She was such a mature and obedient girl. She had told me that until her father changed his mentality, she couldn't attend to my calls.'

'Yah! That's all right. But at present, how can you face her uncle and the others?'

'I don't know. But I want to meet her to tell her something. Our love can't claim any life.'

Shilpa remained silent.

'Okay, Shilpa, if you get any news, don't forget to call me.'

After taking a quick bath, I was ready myself to go to the hospital. I called Sir Monish to accompany me. I told him of the incident. We went on my bike to KIMS hospital in Trivandrum. I rode the bike in such a speed that someone from my own family was hospitalized and in a critical condition. At around eight in the morning, we reached the hospital. I went to the reception counter to enquire about one Mr Nanda Kishore admitted yesterday night from Chavara. The receptionist gave me the admittance details of him: seventh floor, ICU, Room No. 704. As it was visiting time, there was no restriction to go there. We waited in front of the lift numbered 5.

While we waiting for the lift, I saw Nimmy's uncle coming out from one of the lifts and going out to the reception counter. He might be going out for a morning tea or walk. Among the crowds, he could not have noticed me; I too never wanted to come in front of his eyes. Our lift was opened for us, and we occupied it for seventh floor. After two, three halts, it reached the seventh floor, and we alighted there and proceeded to Room 704. The door was left slightly open. I took a peep into it. I saw Nimmy sitting beside the bed, leaning her head on the bed. The dripping of the bathroom tap was the only sound that can be heard there. I felt that the dripping water was a sad background music to her grief. I saw she was alone there.

I gently pushed open the door. She raised her head and saw me. Seeing me, she began to shed tears.

'How is he now?' I asked with a trembling voice.

She gestured a satisfactory sign.

'Sorry, Nimmy.' I was struggling for words to comfort her. What words could comfort her at all? She was in such a depressed state that she couldn't even talk.

Her mother stepped out from the washroom. Looking at me, her face got discoloured. She stared at me for a moment, then asked me, 'How dare you come here? Do you intend to kill all my family?'

'Mum, please . . .' Nimmy pleaded.

'Let your mum speak . . .' I requested of her.

'Did you call him?' Her mum turned to her in fury.

'No, Auntie. Shilpa phoned me just an hour ago. I couldn't tolerate it because I am also involved in the sin.' I explained.

'And you both decided to murder my husband?' she asked, and I had no reply at all. I kept my head downwards.

'Mum . . . don't be harsh.'

'Is this the place and time for your rendezvous with him?'

'Aunt, don't hurt us like that. Really, after the disagreement with Nimmy's father, she never attended my call. This is the first time ever that we have met each other after that. I never expected such an ending of our friendship. I just came to say sorry for you, ma'am. I am on no account requiring anyone in my life after hurting others.'

'Do you know how much she argued for you with her father and how that argument had hurt him more than the disgrace he has to face from his community? Her dad is such a poor man who has never ever scolded his daughters for their faults. How did she have the guts to speak him like that? She had threatened him of suicide if he did not agree to your marriage. Was that the way of speaking to a dad like him?' She sobbed with her words. After a pause, she continued, 'This is pure insolence from her. We can't expect children to behave like this to their own parents.'

As a silent listener, Sir Monish stood in the room the whole time. He broke his silence by asking about the present state of the patient. Nimmy's mummy came down to a tranquil mood after the first reaction, especially because she had heard good news about her husband from the doctors.

'He had lost a lot of blood. The doctors said that the radial artery, the artery in his wrist, would cause shock from the blood loss. It will take at least a week to recover his former strength. I didn't expect such a move from him. In the night at around ten thirty, he went to the bathroom, but even after half an hour, he didn't return. So I went up there to call him. There was no reply, and the tap was running the whole time. I called my children, and when we managed to open the door, he had already collapsed in the bathroom with a pool of blood all around. Then what happened, even I could not remember.'

The ambience of tension was relaxed a little bit by the presence of Sir Monish and his presence of mind.

In the next moment, she became serious. She warned us to leave the room as her relatives might bully us. Was it a considerate mind towards me, or was it that she didn't want to create a scene in the hospital atmosphere? Anyhow, we decided to leave there without creating any trouble to Nimmy and her family.

Nimmy's image of despair rested in my eyes' frames. As I came out of the room, I couldn't actually see the corridor of the hospital just in front of me. Her heartbroken image of anguish and grief hung back in my mind's eye.

She suffered like a woman whose firstborn baby turned blind.

My mind was troubled like a pouring cloud. I couldn't help avoiding sobbing in my heart. I was responsible for all these troubles to her and her family. I realized that love can also produce the emotion of hatred in others' minds. When two hearts love each other, could the entire people around them begin to hate them?

For one moment, I anticipated if I hadn't met her in my life, I could have made my life an easy-going one. My beloved's suffering pulled me back to the hospital. I couldn't go away from the premises of the hospital without consoling her in the grief. I was ready to do anything for her to get her away from her grief.

Somehow we came out of the main entrance of the hospital where there was a queue of vehicles in three lines dropping visitors and patients. We walked along the footpath and proceeded to the front road. I looked back in hopes of seeing her in the waiting room. There was no possibility of getting a glance at the room. It was an inter-block room, and one couldn't get a look at it from any of the surrounding area.

I told Sir Monish my decision to meet her; otherwise, I wouldn't be able to control my sobbing.

He had a class in Excellent Tutorial, so I persuaded him to go and take the class because, on a Sunday, shortage of staff to control the classes might cause anger in Sir Baiju. As it was a Sunday, many parents also might come to pay tuition fees and to meet the teachers. I too had class that day. Thus, I forced him to leave there. After having breakfast at the hospital canteen, I dropped him in the highway road from where he could get a direct superfast bus to Parippally.

I came back and waited at the lounge for hours. From the first lounge of the hospital, one could observe all the visitors of the hospital. During the first two hours, I was eagerly looking for Kavu, who was always supportive of our relation. Now and then, I observed the pharmacy section also for Nimmy's arrival. Going again to the room was not possible as her uncles and almost all their relatives could have already reached the hospital.

At around one thirty in the afternoon, I went for a meal in the hospital canteen. After the meal, I came back in the same spot and waited there. I noticed that some people had reserved spots in the lounge for night wait. Those who did not get rooms and those whose dear ones were in the ICU would wait there in the portico lounge. I too occupied such a portion in one of the corners of the waiting hall.

From four o'clock to five thirty in the afternoon, it was the time for visitors. The rush of the hospital increased at this time. A lot of people were seen waiting for their turn in front of the seven lifts there. They went to see their patients to know about the progress in their condition. There were restrictions for visitors in the IC units. The hospital authorities allowed only one or two visitors to enter the intensive care unit to see the patient. Most people in the waiting lounge left there for the ICU. But I was still waiting there.

The refreshment kiosk woman asked me, 'Don't you want to see your patient?'

'I am not allowed because I have a cold.' I gave her my excuse.

In the evening, Monish rang to enquire about me. I told him that till now it was not possible for me to meet her. She didn't have her mobile with her. In a hurry, she could have forgotten everything. So I was in the hospital even now; he didn't need worry about me.

I felt that time moved on an elephant's back up to a hilltop. Nevertheless, once the night began to draw out it spread like that of the shaking news of the assassination of Indira Gandhi, the former prime minister of India. Each and every dot in the area was covered with darkness. Inside the hospital, there was no change except that some of the bystanders began to narrate their pangs and pains that they were bearing for their dear ones.

One of the women told her floormate in Tamil that night, 'Enre kanavanuk ithana divasukkullil ainch lack rupaya mudichach, kadavul kappathane.' Within these days, she had spent five lakh rupees for her husband. God save us.

Her husband had met with a road accident at Thirunalveli and was brought to this hospital four days earlier. They were sharing their grievances just before they set to sleep. As she lay down with a sigh of relief, an announcement came in English: 'Ramalingam's bystander is needed at ICU, please contact immediately.' It was followed by one in Tamil, and the woman who was talking about her husband immediately woke up and went for the lift.

The loudspeakers were kept in the waiting room counter for the purpose of giving information to patients and bystanders. After a few minutes, a low-voiced announcement came in Sinhala language, which was meant for a Sri Lankan patient's bystander.

I was one among the many bystanders, but I couldn't understand for whom I was staying there. My sole purpose was to meet her, and I wanted to share a part of her pain. I could not bear the pain she was undergoing.

I had my supper at nine in one of the outside hotels and went back to my reserved place.

A middle-aged woman was weeping all the time. A woman near her asked her the reason. She began to narrate her story. Her husband was admitted in the intensive care unit. In the evening, they came to call on his brother who had been admitted in the VICU care centre due to lack of oxygen in his blood. Her husband was just a visitor to the patient, but on seeing the patient's condition, he collapsed there due to a cardiac arrest. He had been admitted in the same ICU for the last five hours.

As she narrated her story, the listener sighed for her.

During one of his night roamings, Nimmy's uncle saw me there in the lounge, but I did not see him. He knew me well, but he in no way thought that I was there to pray for the life of his brother-in-law.

In the casual talk during bedtime between Nimmy's uncle and her mother, he mentioned about my waiting in the lounge.

'Is he still there?' Nimmy's mother asked in anguish.

Till then, he not had been aware of my visit there. 'Have you seen him?'

'In the morning, he came here'

'For what?'

'To enquire about the condition.'

'Who informed him?'

'Shilpa, his classmate.'

They thought Nimmy had already gone to sleep, but she heard it with a shudder in her heart.

With a sob in her heart, she experienced my presence around her. She really felt sorry for me. A deer can't leave its antlers, a flower can't leave its fragrance, a river can't leave its flow of music, the sun can't leave its warmth, the winter can't leave its cold. In the same way, she can't leave me, and I can't leave her. I was not in a sleepy mood today. My sleep was taken away by Nimmy's heart-rending face. I just closed my eyes and thought about Nimmy.

In the middle of the night, a soft and squashy hand caught on my shoulder. I opened my eyes. To my surprise and joy, I recognized Nimmy in the faint light of the hospital portico.

'Nilesh, you didn't go away?'

'No.'

'Why?'

'Tell me how I can when you are in such a . . .?'

'But . . .' She began to sob and embraced me over my shoulder and closed her eyes. I too took her to my bosom and consoled her. I got a fresh life to my soul as she came out for me.

'Let us move out from here.' I gently woke her from the hug. Her eyes were filled with tears. I wiped away her tears.

'Tell me, how is Uncle now?'

'Fine. Better improvement.'

'Did you see him?'

'Yes.'

'Did he speak to you?'

'Not that much better.'

'Where is Kavu?'

'She is in Uncle's house. Had Shilpa phoned you?'

'Yes. The moment I heard, I set out. Why didn't you call me all these three days? How could you, Nimmy?'

'I am helpless, Nilesh. I had never disobeyed my parents. They gave us love that no one could get. They gave me freedom that not anyone could get. Then what did I do to them in return? Can anyone tolerate that?' She began to weep.

I wiped away her tears, which were burning and holy, through which our minds' stains were washed away.

We came out of the entrance gate and went to the front garden of the hospital. We sat on a garden bench there under the palm tree.

'I think after two or three days, he will be shifted to the room.'

'Most probably.'

'You know, we can't live without one another, our existence itself is fixed together. Yet I want to tell you something that may pain us, but it undeniably brings cheer to your parents' faces.'

'What are you telling me, Nilesh?'

'I see only this solution for our relation.'

After a long pause, 'What . . . ?'

'Let us . . . separate . . . forever.' A thunder shock hit my heart as I told this to her.

She put her forehead on her hand and sighed violently. The sighing slowly turned to groaning.

I put my elbow on my knees and enclosed my forehead and cheeks in my hands. She wept so hard that I couldn't even console her because inwardly I was also crying so bitterly.

Till that moment, we thought we were made for each other like a temple and its deity.

But everything collapsed within no time.

A long pause spotted with our weeping filled the air.

'Can you, Nilesh?' She broke the silence.

'We . . . have to. This is the only way we can save your family.'

'How cruel is this fate?' She couldn't control her emotions. Life has to face incredible odds sometimes. Tears were seeping out from the watershed of her heart. Even though the walls of the watershed should be strong enough, the pressure inside it made tears seep through.

'Nimmy, I will come back to meet your father when he is taken to the room. At that time, we can disclose our decision to him. It will make him so happy. He must remain as the most blessed father. Think of him. He is ready to leave his life to get you back. Such a father should not be made to weep anymore. This will be the most blessed thing we can do for him.' During this time, a hot sun was burning in my heart; a life without the blessing of parents, I simply couldn't bear it anymore. I cursed my own life as a sinned one.

We woke from the shock at four in the morning when the milk tempo reached there. I immediately accompanied her back to the room, where her disappearance was not yet noticed.

'Be careful while riding the bike,' she advised me just before parting.

I came back home in a heartbroken condition. I reached there at around five thirty in the morning. I couldn't control my heart's weeping. I went straight to the bed and began to groan terribly.

The cry got its momentum as pain came out of my heart, and the groan became a screaming. I screamed as loud as I could, calling, '*Oh* . . . my mother . . . *I could not help it*, my mother . . .'

Ammini, my woman neighbour, came there, hearing my cry. She asked me what had happened. But her query fell on deaf ears as I was completely ignorant of the situation. A little later, she went away and came back with her husband to find out what had happened to me. As they could not understand the reason for my crying, they sent for Kuttathy Chechi.

At the time Kuttathy Chechi came there, I had lost my voice to crying. She asked me if I needed any medical help. She knew well why I was crying, but to hide this from my neighbours, she told them that nowadays I was suffering from abdominal pain and it had to be checked up in a good hospital.

How could she tell them that the pain was not in the stomach but in the mind? Again, they tried their best to know my problem, but as there was no reply, they left the place after a short while.

A baby cries hard for its mother's cuddling, and when it fails to get it, it goes on crying louder and louder. And in the end, it will go to a deep sleep, a sleep of fatigue, so I cried and went to sleep.

I woke up at three o'clock in the afternoon.

In the duration, no one came there to wake me. After getting freshened up, I went for the first and perhaps last meal of the day in Saji's restaurant. The old country shop was modified a few months back, and a name board was put in front of it. People came there to take homemade food. By the time I reached there, the mealtime was over. Tea and snacks were ready to be served. Vada, *modakam*, and banana fries were cumulated in three basins on the desk for the customer to get a close look and to tempt the tea-taker for a hot snack.

Saji, the hotel owner's son, was my childhood friend. He took me to the inner room and served the meal with the dishes taken from his own house, which was adjacent to the shop. But I couldn't eat much. My appetite was totally dead. I was totally depressed and dejected like a patient with a newly detected cancer. My cancer was on my mind. It was only because of my mother's blessing that I never committed suicide or went mad.

Meanwhile, I thought once again about the very first of the premier feelings of humans—love. Love is really like a rose. It sprouts among the thorns. Its fragrance can't be felt by the plant from which it has blossomed.

After the light meal, I went to meet Kuttathy Chechi. I told her about our decision to separate. It was a divorce before the marriage—not because of our own fault, but because of the disinterest of the fiancée's family and because both of us were born in two different castes of Hindu religion. *A man predestined to live unaccompanied can't change his fate at any circumstances*, my pessimism told me.

CHAPTER 13

On the third day of my separation from Nimmy, I received a message from her: 'Dad taken to room. Fine.'

A long sigh of relief from my heavy heart flew out on a kite to the open air. It brought back a kite full of fresh air from atop. That air cooled and soothed my bereaved heart. I felt I was coming back to normalcy slowly. But I realized that my pain of love couldn't be cured even by the best doctor of the time.

'I need to meet him for Nimmy,' I soliloquized to myself. But how could I? How am I to face him when I was responsible for his mental misery and suicidal attempt? Yet I had to because Nimmy said to.

I took my bike and left home for KIMS at around ten thirty in the morning. While I rode to the hospital to meet Nimmy's family once again in a critical situation, several feelings were aroused in my mind regarding especially facing her father. Throughout the ride, I pictured the scene of what could happen. Within one and half hours, I reached the hospital.

I kept my bike in the back courtyard of the hospital and went to Room 704. I fell into the twilight zone of apprehension and tranquillity. My apprehension was for the meeting, and my tranquillity for giving relief to them. What would be his reaction? The most prominent hesitation arose in my mind. Would it be another shock for him? For a man coming back from the threshold of death, certain changes must have occurred in his mind. He should have the patience to hear me out. As I took assurance in my mind, I tapped on the door.

Kavu opened the door. Seeing me, she immediately withdrew to her mother. Nimmy was sitting on the second bed there. She had a weighty mind; her expression on her face clearly declared this. I felt she was singled out in her familial circle. I entered there and looked at Nimmy's father, who was lying on the patient bed. As he saw me, he gave me a 'What do you want?' look. But I looked at him in a pleading way to permit me to speak.

'I'm not asking about your health. I am so sorry for all that happened. Now I am before you to inform our joint decision. Uncle, you need not do any more attempts to commit this sin. I know your children love you like you are the most lovable father in the whole world. They can't survive without you. So we took a joint decision to surrender our love before you for the well-being of your health . . . and for your long life.' I paused. 'We will *never* . . . meet again . . . *I promise* . . . in our entire lives.' A sob chocked me, and three drops of tears fell down from my crammed eyes.

Nimmy put her head down; she shed tears on her lap, and Kavu turned her head away in sorrow.

'But you should have shown a little more humanity. At least, that much we have shown,' I continued. I turned to Nimmy's mother. 'Auntie, are you happy now? I am giving you back your daughter. I came here just to convey this message to you. Now the fire in my heart has been lost. Remember, Uncle, suicide is not a remedy. It is a punishment for us. Your daughter doesn't do anything without your permission, even the decision of her marriage. She will be innocent as always. Now, I am leaving . . . leaving . . . forever.' After saying this, I turned to the door.

'Son,' Nimmy's mother called me back.

I turned to look at her.

'Don't misunderstand us. Don't do any unwanted thing on this matter like my husband did.' After saying this, she hunted for something from the tabletop. She took a pen and extended it towards me and said, 'This is a simple gift for you for your good will. Keep it with you, son.'

The real gift they had taken back and now was giving me a memorial endowment.

I received it from her and came out of the room. But I did not have any guts to look at Nimmy, my sweetheart. I controlled all my feelings although a tsunami of memories flooded my mind, but I had to control them all without causing any damage to the shores of my simple and lonely heart. I would miss Nimmy forever in my entire life. Now it was opened to the entire world. I felt grief over all the people I had met and all the things I had looked at. Everything lamented with me. Even my bike refused to start at first. The coconut trees bowed down their long leaves to join me in my grief.

I could not remember my ride back home from KIMS. As I entered my bedroom, I collapsed on to my cot. For three hours, I had a continuous suppressed cry like a dear one in my family had died and all hope for a comeback had been lost forever.

The next day, our final results were published. Nimmy and I got first place in the exam. I remained the topper from my college. She secured the second position with seven marks less from me in the grand total. The main thing was both of us qualified to attempt the UGC test. The results brought no happiness to us. Nimmy didn't call me, nor I her. There was absolute zero communication between us. Everything was frozen in between us like a huge past. We were on no man's land.

CHAPTER 14

Love is like rain. It comes with a lot of sweet dreams and later flows away, leaving a lot of sorrows. The chill of sweet dreams left with the flow. What remains is the raw life to sprout a new beginning.

Even after the ninth day of separation, I could not control my mind. I felt I needed some spiritual support to sustain my mind. A comrade's mind needed some spiritual support for survival. The ebb and flow of emotions began to disturb me. I decided to visit Guruvayur Temple to pray. I told the same to my uncle and a few friends to avoid any unnecessary speculations on my disappearance because it took three days to complete the pilgrimage.

I booked an e-ticket in the Guruvayur–Punalur Express. It was a Saturday. At around 9 p.m., I reached the Kollam Junction Railway Station on platform no. 3. The station was deserted like an after-festival temple; only a few passengers were waiting here and there for the train. Mine was coach no. S5. At nine thirty, the announcement for the train was heard. I got ready for boarding. The train was on time. As I entered and found my berth, which was an upper one, I climbed up with the backpack. I cleaned the berth with a piece of newspaper and spread my sheet on it. I found my perception of god began to amend. I opened the Rail Neer bottle and gulped down the last of the water in it.

Yes, a drop of water causes the beginning of a life, and before its end as well, we do the same thing. I began to pray for the ultimate aim of peace of mind.

At around ten thirty, the TTR came to check the tickets.

I asked him, 'At what time will it reach at Guruvayur Temple?'

'At two thirty in the early morning,' he replied very reluctantly.

A family of devotees had already occupied the other berths in the room. I lay down on my berth. As I lay down, my mind flew back to memories of Nimmy. The name itself was a launching pad of innumerable flashbacks in my life. I could not delete it from the hard disk of my brain. It kept open several active windows in my mind.

I did not know at what time I went to sleep. I woke up at the commotion of co-passengers when the train reached Guruvayur Station. From the station, I went straight to Devasom Inn and took a room for my bathing and primary needs. After a quick bath, I went for the devotee queue in the temple for the holy darshan. Already a long line stretching out to the entrance gate of the temple was seen there. I also took a place in the queue. The long queue began to move at around four in the early morning with the beginning of *neeranjanam* offering. The queue was moving forward like driving in a heavy traffic jam. Within half an hour, I entered the sanctum sanctorum of the Krishna temple.

Just after I prayed to Lord Krishna, the security men forced me to move forward. In the rush, I landed in front of the most cherished gift. I felt like I really saw the Lord

Krishna in front of me. I saw her, my sweetheart in front of my eyes. I could not believe my eyes. I thought I was in a wild dream. The moment I looked at her, she turned and looked at me. Both of us were paralyzed in that unexpected encounter and looked at each other for a while. Perhaps she remembered the same thing as I remembered at this moment of unforeseen meeting the words I gave to her father: 'Never ever in our lives will we meet again.' Then what happened now? We both were stuck in the thought, 'Was it a god-destined meeting?' We were amazed.

We became conscious of each other. We understood the pain we were bearing in our minds. Our faces were so heavy like our minds.

Nimmy's parents were with her. They might have also come for the same purpose like mine—for a divine relief for their grieving hearts. The difference between them and me was that they shared the grief among themselves but I was carrying it all alone. The misery was easily visible in my face and posture.

Her parents turned back and called her. They saw me too. They could not believe their eyes. For a moment, they were astonished. They stared at me with the looks of 'How did he come here?' 'How did he come to know about our pilgrimage to Guruvayur?' 'Did she inform him?' And a lot of doubts arose in their looks. Their look showed me all these pop-up screens on their faces.

I put a few steps forward and told them, 'It was not a deliberate deed. I am a communist by belief, yet I find this is the only way to get solace for my mind. Sorry . . . I never expected that you would also be here in front of Lord Krishna.'

My unshaven face and trembling voice might have made them pity me. I turned to Nimmy and asked, 'Are you fine . . . Nimmy?'

'How are you, Nilesh?' Her reply was another question. 'Congrats for your first position in our class.' She used the moment to congratulate me. Her heart was burning to talk about something with me like a devotee unexpectedly seeing her favourite god in front of her.

'Ehhhhhh . . .' My eyes fell on hers. I never expected such a meeting with her in that faraway place in the holy land of Lord Krishna's temple.

I had changed a lot in the past few days. I had not even shaven my face for the last few days. My mind's numbness was expressed on my face. Totally, I bore a shaggy look. When Nimmy saw me, she was completely disturbed. She knew me well than anyone else in my life. She looked at me, and she observed me as a mother who had found her lost son after a few months of separation. She wanted to come and hug me, but the sense of her parents being against us, and I am a forbidden lover prevented her from doing it.

Unexpectedly, Nimmy came forward and kneeled before her father with a request. 'Dad, could you . . . please . . . let me marry him? I can no longer bury my heart. Otherwise, I may go mad. Pleaseeeeeeeeee . . .' she pleaded so hard with tears crammed in her eyes that dropped on the sanctum sanctorum of Lord Krishna's temple.

My heart broke into little pieces like a meteor collision took place in the space. I shut my eyes and cried, 'Oh my god, oh Maa . . .'

I felt like the whole temple, with all its devotees and deity in it, was moving around me. I woke up from the panorama on hearing a loud call.

'Hey, Mr Nilesh, come here,' Nimmy's father commanded me. I went to him.

'Do you know after your departure, we lost our dear daughter? She is not the one that we expected you to return. We want our old Nimmy. Can you give our old daughter back?'

He lifted up her daughter from his feet and consoled her. He patted her head and wiped the tears and said, 'From this holy land, I extend my permission for your reunion. I really subdued all my pride before your love.'

He put her hands on mine.

I could not believe my senses; I could not comprehend what was going on there. I was absolutely stunned in his change.

When I came back to sanity, I seized Nimmy's hands and went back to the shrine of the temple and prayed with a serene mind. She looked at my eyes itself. We heaved off all our worries on to the holy shrine. The love match thanked the lord for creating the background for their reunion.